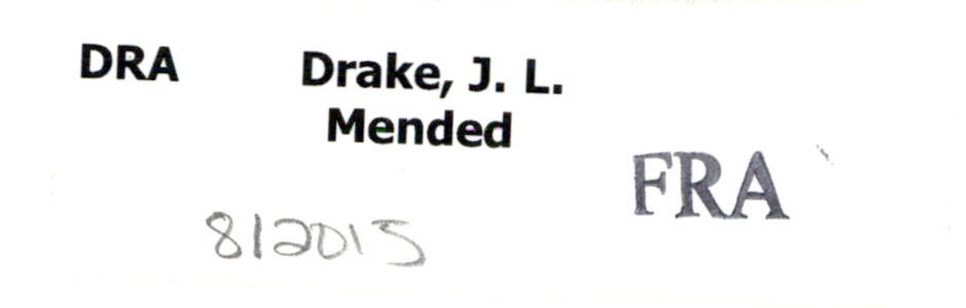

Mended

Broken Trilogy, Book Three

J.L. Drake

Mended

First Print Edition: June 2015

Limitless Publishing, LLC
Kailua, HI 96734
www.limitlesspublishing.com

Formatting: Limitless Publishing

ISBN-13: 978-1-68058-154-6
ISBN-10: 1-68058-154-6

This is a work of fiction. Names, characters, places, and incidents either are the product of the author's imagination or are used fictitiously, and any resemblance to locales, events, business establishments, or actual persons—living or dead—is entirely coincidental.

Dedication

Mom,
Our journey in life will test us,
mold us, and define us.
We've been broken and shattered,
but now we are mended.
Now is the time to live.
Now is the time for happily ever after.
Enjoy.

Baby Olivia,
Run for two, love for two, live for two.
~ Aunt Jodi

Prologue

They say time heals all wounds, but they fail to mention it's a bitch of a journey.

I'm twenty-nine years old and feel I haven't really lived yet. My life up to now has been filled with lies, loss, death, betrayal, and heartache. After several months of hell, I'm finally over the worst of it, and now I'm starting to mend, slowly pulling my life together and picking up the pieces.

It's time to live…my way…

Chapter One

Savannah

I close the door behind Keith, and watch him disappear down the hallway. I lock the two deadbolts, chain, and latch, and breathe a sigh of relief. Keith installed them all the night I arrived, while I pretended to act like I was fine without them. *Not true*. He spoke with the man at the front desk about keeping an eye on me, and also put sensors on all my windows…I live on the fifth floor.

After I grab a quick bite to eat, I head over to the mirror, checking my outfit and smoothing my hands over my hair. *I can do this*. I pick up my keys after a little mental pep talk and head out, pushing myself to move forward. The painfully slow elevator calls me, but I opt for the stairs instead. It's been a week since I left the safe house and moved here, a week since I've seen Cole. Keith keeps finding odd jobs around my one-bedroom apartment that he can only do during the night, since he has to work through the day. I know he's nervous to leave me alone, and frankly, I like having him on my couch. Of course I keep telling him to leave and stop babying me, but that's just another lie I add to the already long list.

Secretly, I'm worried my friends back at the safe house are growing tired of me, so I'm trying to act as independent as possible. That's why I'm walking three blocks to Zack's restaurant, knowing that Keith is sitting in the coffee shop across the street, watching me to make sure I get there all right. I smile to myself and pull out my sunglasses. Who knew scary old Keith would end up being a protective older brother?

I grin, thinking about the other day.

My apartment is quiet, something I don't enjoy anymore. Melanie is out with friends and wanted me to join them, but all I want to do is watch old reruns of Lie to Me. Maybe I'll learn something. Resting my glass of wine on my leg, I pull the covers over me more. It's cold, and I'm too stubborn to turn up the heat. I don't want my electric bill to be too much. Daniel is trying to pay my bills, but I'm determined not to have that happen. I'll be making enough when I start my new job in a few days. I don't need much.

I'm not sure what time it is when a light knocking wakes me. Oh, wow, I must have dozed off. I pull my lazy ass off the couch and trudge to the door, looking through the peephole to find Keith staring back at me.

After I unlock all five locks, I open the door. He is holding a plastic bag.

"I got you a fish."

What?

He holds up the bag, showing me a purple rainbow fish staring back at me through the plastic.

Ewww.

"Why?"

I hate fish.

He smiles, seeing my discomfort. "'Cause you're lonely and could use someone you can't push away." He steps past me, but turns when I go to close the door. "Wait."

"I don't push people away." I fold my arms as I look down the hallway and wonder who else is coming.

"Right." He chuckles as he runs water into a glass bowl he took from another bag. "You'd be surprised how attached you can become to Aloof, *here."*

I shake my head. "Aloof?"

He nods as he slips the fish into its new home. "Seems suitable for how you've been lately."

I close my eyes, feeling his words hit me like a blow to the gut. "I'm sorry, Keith. I'm not trying to push anyone away. Especially not you. I-I...don't know what I am."

He sits the bowl on my counter, rubbing his finger along the glass and getting the fish's attention.

"I know things have been rough lately. Just don't shut us all out." I nod miserably. The cookies are on top of the fridge. I reach up and grab them and sit them in front of him.

"Truce?"

"I was never mad at you. I just miss the old Savannah sometimes." He takes my hand and drags me into a side hug, while he snags two cookies at once. "Do you need anything?"

I shrug, knowing he needs this. "Actually, the tap in the bathroom has been dripping."

His face lights up. "I'll go get my tools."

"Wait, Keith, who is comin—"

"Why does your elevator take nine years to get to the fifth floor?" June jokes, setting a large box on my kitchen table. I nearly jump into her arms. I'm so thankful to see family here in my own place.

June nods at Abigail, who is holding a bag full of homemade food.

"Thought you might like something different to eat." She opens my fridge and sees my jar of peanut butter and bottled water. "Well, I thought you might be hungry."

"Thanks!" I peer over her shoulder and see a container of her lentil soup. Yum.

June pours herself a glass of wine, then wanders over to the couch and retrieves mine from the side table. "This is a lovely place, dear."

"Thank you." I sit at the counter and watch Abigail.

"Here," Abigail says, pushing a large wrapped present toward me. "This is to keep Keith happy."

I grin, wondering what the heck it can be. I pluck the silver bow off and rip the paper down the sides. My hands stop mid-tear when I see what it is. "Oh my."

"I hope it's the right color."

"It is." I open the box and carefully pull it free

from all the packaging. My fingers run along the red paint, down the neck, and around the shiny metal bowl. "It's just like her Mixmaster." Pressing my lips together, I rein in my emotions. How did I ever get so lucky to have these two amazing women in my life? "Thank you so much!"

"You're more than welcome, dear." They both give me a hug.

It looks perfect next to my coffee maker. I turn to see June and Abigail looking at my living room. Leaning against the counter, I feel happy they're here. This is nice. I really have to try harder.

***

"This is your locker, aprons are here, bathrooms are over there, and this is where you punch in and out." Zack takes the time card and slips it into the slot where we hear it stamp the long yellow form. "There, you're officially on the clock." He motions for me to follow him through a short hall to the bar which is alongside his restaurant. "Since you've bartended before, this shouldn't be too hard for you. Jake will show you the ropes."

"All right." Butterflies dance in my stomach. I'm nervous about being around such a large crowd; it's been a while.

He hands me my nametag. "Here's the deal, Savi. You have any problems with the customers, talk to Jake. He's great, and he'll have your back no matter what. We don't have much trouble here, but there are always a few…well, you know what I mean. But if *Savannah* needs help," he gives me a look to make sure I understand that I go to him if something comes up with my case, "you come find me. I should always be working the same shift as you, but if for some reason I'm not, Keith or Daniel won't be far away. Any questions?" I shake my head, taking it all in. "Jake," he calls out, "meet your new sidekick."

A tall, well-built guy about my age flashes me a set of pearly whites. "Well, aren't I just the lucky one? Hey there, I'm Jake."

"Savi." We shake hands, but before I pull away, he spins me around, studying me.

"Okay, first, this isn't going to work." He shakes his head and reaches under the bar and hands me a t-shirt. "Go put this on." He smiles and points to a small door. I quickly change into a black V-neck t-shirt that has a bit more cleavage showing than something I would have picked out. The shirt hangs just below my belly button, showing half an inch of skin above my pants. Jake rubs his fingers over his lips when he sees me. "Good, but…" he pulls my ponytail free and lets my hair fall around my shoulders, "this is better." He nods approval. "Sex sells, and in the afternoon and night this place is buzzing with tired men looking for a drink. With that body and face, Savi, we'll have this place packed to the max, and that means…tips!"

Just after seven, the place is slammed. Thankfully, Jake is patient, and my memory hasn't given up on me. I've never made four apple martinis at once, but I'll tell you what, I can now. I learn quickly that the girls who come to the bar are rich and impatient, and most of the men are into some kind of extreme sport or other. I barely have time to think about breathing before the next order is being barked at me, but I'm soon into the swing of it and am getting the job done.

"You have a gentleman caller," Jake says over my shoulder as I enter the order into the computer.

I glance over and see Mark grinning as he snags an empty seat in the middle of the bar. I finish up and head over, wiping my hands on a rag.

"Well, hello, stranger," I lean over and give him a hug. "It's good to see your face."

He eyes my shirt. "He's not going to like this." That painful knot in my stomach tightens, but I shrug his comment off. "How are you, Savi?"

I laugh and lean over the counter to make my point. "Really, how am I?" *Like you all don't get a play by play update from Keith.* He smirks, nodding at the Stella on tap. I grab a glass and pour him one. "I'm all right, but I'd be lying if I said I didn't miss you guys. How are things at the house? How's Abby? Is June still here?"

"You can come home, you know." He peers at me over his glass, but when he sees my shrug he changes the topic. "June is still here. She's talking about moving in permanently. She hates being away from her sister. You know how she and Abby are," he smiles.

I slap my rag against the counter. "Really? It will be so great to have her around!"

"Yeah, it will be." He turns his attention to a customer who's calling out for me. I hold up a finger and rush over to the guy.

"Hi, what can I get you?" I ask.

The man pushes up his sleeves as he takes a seat. "You, for starters." I sigh inwardly and keep my expression the same.

"How 'bout a drink?" I counter, but this makes him smile.

"Scotch, neat, keep them coming, and if by the end of the night you do a good job, I'll do the same for you." He slips me his credit card and hotel key. I stare at them both in shock. This man doesn't waste any time. I pluck the credit card and, ignoring his key, make his drink. When I hand him the drink, he wraps his fingers around mine. "I'm Don." He reaches over with his free hand and fingers my nametag. "Savi, that's a pretty name."

"Thanks," I say, pulling my hand away. "Excuse me." I head back over to Mark, who is watching me like a hawk. I slap on a smile and ask if he wants another.

"Really, Savi, you want to work here? With *these* guys?" Mark twists his beer in his hand as he points with his head at the Don guy. "Cole isn't going to like this."

Shaking my head, hands on my hips, I raise an eyebrow at him. "Were you sent here to spy, Mark, or did you come by as a friend seeing a friend?"

He glares right back. "First, I'm seeing family, not just a friend. You don't think I'll be hounded when he calls in tonight? Please spare me the look. I have to report something to the poor guy."

I reach for a towel and wipe down a nonexistent water ring. "Where is he this time?"

"Washington. He testified against The American yesterday." My throat suddenly goes dry. "It went well. He should be home tonight or tomorrow." He makes a face, and I know what he's going to say.

"When do I have to go?" The blood drains from my face when I think about having to see those people again.

Mark downs his beer. "Cole is trying to get you out of it. We're hoping you can do it from here using video chat, but it would be more effective if you were there in person."

"I'll do it," I say, tossing the towel aside. "Tell Frank I'll come to Washington."

"You don't have to, Sav—"

"I should get back to my customers. It was really nice seeing you, Mark. Please say hello to everyone for me." I start to walk away, but Mark hooks my arm and stops me.

"Come by the house tomorrow night and have dinner with us."

I shake my head. "Sorry, I'm working."

"Then during the day?"

"I'll see," I pat his arm and leave to tend to the rest of the customers.

"You did great tonight," Jake says a few hours later as he tugs the strap of his bag over his head. "Can I walk you out?"

"Sure." We step out into the freezing air, and tiny snowflakes wander down from the sky. I wrap my scarf around my neck. "How long have you been working for Zack?"

Jake starts walking in my direction. "For about three years. I don't have any family here, so he's taken me under his wing. I see he's done the same with you." I nod, feeling very at ease with Jake.

He's very kind and soft spoken. "Actually, you seem to have a lot of people keeping an eye on you," he says quietly. "That guy who came by tonight, is he your boyfriend?"

"Just a close friend," I smile, thinking if Mark came off as my boyfriend, maybe Don will lay off the next time he comes in for a drink.

"That's good, because I know he's dating Mel." I glance up at him. "She's a friend too. So what's the deal, Savi? You have Mark, Zack, and that huge, tall guy who's like your shadow."

"Keith," I say with a laugh. "He's like an older brother."

"Okay, so what's with the army of men? You, like, in some kind of trouble?" I nearly trip on flat ground with his guess.

"You're pretty observant for only knowing me for, what, nine hours?"

He pulls the collar of his jacket up higher to keep the chill off his neck. "It's sorta something I do. I love to people watch." He stops and turns to face me. "I'm just offering an ear if you need it." He points with his head. "This is me." I smile when I see we are standing in front of my building.

"What floor?"

His face drops. "Oh—ah…I didn't mean…"

I grin when I realize how that just sounded. "I meant what floor, because I live on the fifth."

He tosses his head back, laughing. "I'm in 5G."

"5H." I extend a hand. "Nice to meet you, neighbor."

We take the stairs, bitching about the elevator, and saying goodbye outside our doors. Once inside,

I check my phone, which is on the counter where I left it. I keep forgetting I own one now. Two missed calls from Keith and a text letting me know he won't be spending the night.

My stomach twists when I realize I'll be on my own for the first time since moving here. My finger taps the counter as I re-read the message. I guess I'm going to have to get used to this. It is what I wanted. I text him back saying I'm home and no problem.

After a long shower, I still can't seem to unwind, even though the water felt wonderful. I pull on yoga pants and a tank top and lie in bed, pulling the covers to my chin. I find myself staring at the ceiling, wishing I could stop jumping at everything that goes bump in the night.

Tears leak out as I think of Cole. I wonder if he's thinking of me. Probably not in the way I'd want. I want to call him so badly to find out if he really meant those words, but I can't. I can't show weakness; I have to stay strong. I stroke absently along the spot next to me, feeling the coldness of the sheets there, and jerk my hand back. I curl into a ball and let my armor flake away. Oh, I miss him so much. I would do anything to smell him right now. Then I remember something, and my feet hit the cold wood floor, hurrying my steps. Yanking open the top right drawer, I see it tucked neatly inside. I remove my tank top and pull on Cole's camo t-shirt. His name, Logan, wraps around my back almost like it's his arm. Looking around my room, I decide this just won't do, so I grab my comforter and pillow. Instead of going back to bed, I head out to the living room where I click on the TV and make myself comfy on the couch facing the door. I spend the next four hours watching reruns of Fresh Prince of Bel-Air.

At nine in the morning, I hear a knock at the door. Keith always texts when he's in the building. Standing on my tiptoes, I peek through the peephole and laugh, opening the door to Jake standing in a pair of fleece PJ pants holding an empty mug, his blond hair pointing every which way.

"I smell coffee," he moans like he's still asleep.

Opening the door wider, I let him in. "Are you sleepwalking?" I joke as I lock all five locks behind him.

His eyes are still slits, but I see him take in my bed on the couch and Cole's shirt. "If I am, will you still share that delicious smelling coffee?"

"Come on," I laugh, waving him toward the kitchen. Jake plunks down on a bar stool as I move about, fixing us each a cup. "Cheers." I clink my mug to his, and he grins as he sips the brew.

"Sweet Lucifer down in hell, what is this?" At first I think he's being insulting, but his face says otherwise.

I lean my hip into the counter and give him a look. "I add a little something to the coffee."

"Savi, I hope you realize what you did," he says with a smirk. "From now on you are now my morning date."

I smile. *See, Savi, progress*. Jake and I spend the rest of the day camped out under the warmth of my comforter. I'm totally at ease with him. He's never once made me feel uncomfortable, and I figure if

Zack trusts him, I can. We order pizza and watch a marathon of Louie CK standups until an hour before our shift starts. Keith texts a few times, and I assure him I'm fine, because I am…at the moment. I've made a friend.

"Savi, can I ask you something?" Jake says, taking a wet napkin to his greasy fingers. "Who's Logan?" I'm thrown by his question until he points to the back of my shirt. *Oh*. "Looks like a legit army shirt, and I'm guessing you're not in the force."

"He's—was my boyfriend," I stumble, feeling that knife to the heart.

Jake nods and shifts so he faces me. "Was it serious?" I nod. "Is he still around?"

"Yeah, it just ended recently, so it's still raw." My voice is barely a whisper.

He smiles, leaning his chin on his hand. "You love him, don't you?"

"I do."

"It sucks to love someone but not be with them." He sighs.

I feel like he may be referring to something in his life, but I don't pry. "Yeah, it does."

"Why do I feel like you have quite the history, Savannah…?" He waits for my last name, but I hesitate. He watches me for a moment. I can see him thinking, then his whole face brightens. "All right, no more prying today. We have to get to work. I'll be waiting for you outside your door in forty-five. For the love of god, do something with that hair of yours!" He laughs and snags another piece of pizza as he heads out the door.

We make it to work on time and the day passes

quickly.

"You two look great!" Zack shouts, slapping his hands together. Jake and I are practicing our bar flare, and find we make a pretty good team. "Oh, Jake, your father called again." As Jake's face goes white, Zack quickly adds, "I told him you don't work here anymore."

"Okay," is all Jake says in reply. *So, Jake has a story too.*

The phone buzzes in my pocket, but I don't take time to look at it because I have a whole snowboard team taking up a table near the window. I grab the iPad and hurry over for the order. Thankfully, they all want the same thing, six pitchers of Bud Light. Once they are looked after, I head back to the counter where Don from last night is downing a scotch, neat.

Jake gives me an annoyed expression and hands me the guy's receipt. "The creep wants *you.* He was pissed I made his first drink, because apparently you can fuck up pouring scotch into a glass…jackass."

I roll my eyes, agreeing, but it's all part of the business.

"Don," I say with zero emotion, "would you like another?"

He licks his lips as he stares at my breasts. "Yes, I sure would." He holds out his glass, and when I reach for it, he runs his free hand up my arm. "Such a pretty woman."

Stepping away and getting a new glass from the bar, I turn my back while I pour. A strange feeling prickles up my spine. I look around, then freeze as I see Cole standing by the door watching. He's in a dark dress shirt and pants, his suit jacket hanging off his arm. Slowly approaching the bar top, he leans on the counter. All the while his eyes burn through me.

"You gonna drink that, or am I?" Don's arrogant voice breaks through the pull Cole has on me. I sit his drink in front of him and reach out to the bar top for support.

Cole pulls at his tie, undoing it, and tosses it on the counter near my hand. I resist the urge to hold it up to my nose and draw in his intoxicating scent. Instead I just pour him a brandy from the top shelf and sit it in front of him as I slowly raise my eyes to meet his stare.

"Thank you." He nods and takes a long sip from the glass.

I muster up all my strength and try to act like his presence isn't affecting my body. "Were you away?" I pick up the rag and dry a non-existent spill.

"I just came back from Washington," he sighs, rubbing his head.

"Have you been home yet?" The words fall from my mouth.

"No, I haven't been *home* yet." His eyes met mine, holding me captive, his mouth wet from the brandy.

"You just needed a drink?"

He shakes his head. "Old habits die hard." His eyes drop to my lips, and everything in my body begs me to lean forward. My tongue darts out as my lips scream for moisture. If we were alone right now, I know I'd give in.

"Sweetie, could I order some food?" Don asks, obviously irritated he's not getting any attention. I close my eyes and try to snap out of this bubble. I turn to find Don waving a menu at me. "I'll take a medium rare steak, with fries and a side of slaw."

"Anything else?"

He reaches in his back pocket, pulls out something, and leans forward, tucking his hotel room key in my cleavage. I toss it on the counter as I turn away, only to hear him chuckle. "You'll give in to me soon, sweetheart."

The mirror in front of me catches Cole's murderous expression, but he stays in his chair.

Throughout the evening, Cole never leaves his stool, barely speaking to me, just observing. Don is extra flirty, which is extremely annoying. Jake is busy but asks if I want Zack to escort Don out. I say no because he's already dropped at least two hundred in the last two nights. I can handle myself.

"Thirty minutes," Jake calls out to me, which means bed in sixty-five. "Are you going to get any sleep tonight?"

"What?" I spin around on my heel.

"Come on, Savi, sleeping on your couch and your eyes puffy from crying. Don't lie to me, girl, I know lack of sleep when I see it." I sneak a glance at Cole, who is, of course, still watching and listening to us.

"Logan," a voice calls out, and Keith takes a seat next to Cole.

Jake catches my eye, looks with one eyebrow raised at Cole, points a finger at him, then slowly moves it to me. "Ohhh, seriously?" I pull on his arm to get him to stop, pleading with him to shut up. He grins in a boyish way and gives me a slow wink. "I'll go punch out for us."

"Thanks," I mutter, trying to tone down the blush I know must be there. I turn to wipe down the bar and see Zack approaching us, smiling at the guys as he gets closer.

"Savi, you're doing great! Everyone loves you here." Zack comes around the bar, high-fiving me. "I heard one of the customers is being a bit of a handful."

"Nothing I can't handle," I assure him.

"Who?" Keith asks Zack, ignoring me.

Zack leans against the bar. "He's a monthly, works for a sports magazine. Bit of a jerk, but nothing to worry about. Besides Jake is watching over her, so she'll be fine."

Cole gets up and walks behind the counter to wash out his glass only inches from me. I can feel his warmth, and I sneak in a quick breath as I give in to the addiction of his scent. As soon as the smell attacks my senses, I have to walk away. It's like a kick straight to the gut. I head out back to my locker to grab my coat and change from my flats to my boots. I sink down onto the bench, feeling just how tired I am. The three-block walk home seems like ten.

"I don't like you working here." Cole's body fills the doorway. He looks concerned as he leans his weight into the wall.

I stand and fling my bag over my shoulder. "I'll be fine."

I hear him sigh. “Savi—”

I don’t want to talk about us right now; I’m too tired. “Do I have to testify in Washington?”

He pushes off the wall and takes a few steps toward me. I grip the strap on my bag to stop myself from reaching out to touch him. “Yes.” My stomach sinks at that three letter word, and I press my teeth into my lower lip as my chin begins to tremble.

“When?” I ask and stare at the floor.

“Not sure yet, but Frank wants you there two days before so he can prep you.” His shoes come into view. He’s so close, and I can’t think when he’s this near.

“You’ll be testifying against Lynn too.” This time my eyes flick up to his. I wasn’t ready for this. I still haven’t dealt with the fact my best friend is the mastermind behind my kidnapping, the one who had a threesome with my father and a man I considered an uncle. My hand flies to my stomach as the room starts to tilt, and he reaches out to stabilize me. I step back, just needing a minute. “Let me touch you,” he whispers.

“I can’t.”

“Why?”

“I’ll fall.” I move around him and make my way back into the bar where Zack is talking with Keith, but I do catch his hiss.

“We’ve talked about that before.”

“Savi, why didn’t you come by the house today? I waited for your call. I could have come and got you.” Keith pulls on his jacket. “I almost came to get you anyway when I got your one-word text.”

“Laundry,” I answer, then grab my tips from the

bar and shove them in my pocket. It's a lousy lie, but I'm too tired to think of anything more to say. "I'll see you tomorrow, Zack," I wave and head for the door.

Jake is waiting outside the door with a strange expression on his face, but as he sees how tired I am, he throws on a smile. His eyes move up over my shoulder before I hear Cole call out for me.

"Let me drive you back," Cole says, coming up behind me and buttoning up his jacket. "It's freezing."

It is freezing, and my hands are already ice, but I have to be strong. Other people who left Shadows don't have the Army driving them home after their night shift. "No, thanks. I find it helps me wind down." *Another lie.* "Besides, Jake is waiting." I point over my shoulder.

Cole glances at Jake, then at me. I can tell he's not happy but not fighting me on it…that's interesting. He steps forward and pulls off his scarf, wrapping it around my bare neck. I struggle not to immediately bury my nose and soak up the scent as he tucks a lose piece of hair behind my ear.

"Text Keith or me when you get home," he whispers, then steps away as I slowly turn to face Jake, who is looking off, trying to give us some privacy.

I pull out the key and open the door to my brightly lit apartment. I've been leaving a light on so it feels like I'm coming home to someone. Once all the doors are locked, I toss my keys in a bowl and head for the shower, then change into Cole's t-shirt and slip into an already made bed on the couch, facing the door. I'm so tired my eyes close immediately, but I only manage to get twenty minutes of sleep before something creaks in my bedroom, making my eyes pop open. I grab my cell from my bag and text Keith that I am home. I find myself writing a text to Cole too.

Savi: Home.

It pings a moment later.

Cole: Did you just get home?

Savi: No, I fell asleep.

Cole: Why aren't you asleep now?

I hesitate, then go with the truth.

Savi: Heard something, it was nothing.

Cole: Something like what?

Savi: Just a noise, but it was nothing.

Cole: Are you able to get back to sleep?

Savi: Yes.

Cole: Text me if you can't.

I pause, my thumb hovering over the send button.

Savi: I miss you.

I slowly delete each letter one by one.

Savi: Thanks, goodnight.

I want to text him to come over, but I don't. Instead I stare at the ceiling until I can't take it anymore. Turning on the TV for company, I decide I might get a cat just so I have something to cuddle up to. Aloof isn't really cutting it. I look over at the fish floating perfectly still and staring at me.

I muster up the courage and creep into my bedroom and grab the little army bear Daniel and Sue bought me for my baby. Suddenly feeling an overwhelming sadness, I cling to it as I watch Friends until the sun comes up.

Chapter Two

My eyelids feel like lead as I force my aching body up off the couch to let in Jake, who is knocking at my door. It's nine a.m. Giving me a once-over, he slips into my apartment holding a laptop with his "just be happy I'm not a twin" coffee cup balanced on top. I find it kind of cute that he always brings his own mug.

"I'd ask how you slept, but it's pretty obvious you're on night two of no sleep." Jake settles onto *his* stool in my kitchen. I pour him a cup and one for myself. I can't wait for the creamy liquid to hit my tongue. Lord, I love coffee. "I want to ask you something, Savi, but I don't want you getting mad at me."

"Okay," I mumble, cracking four eggs into a frying pan. I pull out some fresh chopped peppers, onion, ham, and cilantro and sprinkle them into the pan, adding a little grated cheese and spice. I glance over my shoulder when he doesn't continue and see him typing away on his laptop, so I decide to wait him out. When the omelets are finished, I divide them onto two plates and set them on the counter. They might not be fancy, but they look pretty good. Besides, I need protein badly; caffeine just won't cut it.

"Is this you?" he says suddenly, turning the laptop around, showing a news article with a picture of my father and me with a dramatic crack down the middle and the headline "Rumor Mayor Fox Hired Cartel to Kidnap Own Daughter." I want to vomit, but instead I pick up my fork and cut into the egg. As soon as my tongue touches the Jell-O-like substance it rejects it, and I spit it out, very unladylike, on my plate. Hopping to my feet and shoving my dish in the sink, I lean on the counter with my back to him.

"So I'll take that as a yes," he whispers, closing his laptop.

Tears! Stupid tears are flowing down my cheeks. I blame part of it on lack of sleep. I stand staring at the counter and hear him come up behind me.

"Savi." He reaches for my shoulder and turns me so I'll face him. He smiles at me, holding both my hands. "I didn't mean to upset you. I just knew you looked familiar, and when I heard your name and saw the SWAT type guys watching over you, well, I went with my hunch."

"I-I can't talk about it," I admit, shocking myself with my honestly.

He closes his eyes and presses his lips together, taking a moment to think, then stares down at me. "When I was sixteen, my father came home early from work to find me and his boss's kid having sex on the couch."

"Okay," I murmur, thinking that would be embarrassing.

"It was the first time he ever laid a hand on me, and he beat me until I stopped moving. He threatened my life if I ever saw *Eddy* again." My heart breaks at that moment. His father is an asshole too; he didn't love him for who he was. All the vibes I have about Jake make sense now. He never hit on me because he is gay. "I play the single hottie from L.A. because it works for me. The women pay good money to see this ass in jeans." He laughs darkly and points at his butt. "But if they knew the truth, Zack would lose a lot of regulars, and I'd never do that to him. Zack's too important to me. He's the only one who knows the real me, and now you do too." He sighs and gives me a wink. "A secret for a secret."

I smile through my tears. "Thank you, for being a friend when I really need one." I lean forward, giving him a hug.

Jake and I decide to head to the mall for some decorations to brighten my place up a little. We take his Prius, since it has started snowing again, small flakes, which I know means we're in for a lot of accumulation. The mall is quiet and looks like Cupid threw up all over it. I hate Valentine's Day. I forgot malls decorate weeks before the actual event. After Jake drags me to every candle, picture, pillow, and kitchen store, we walk out of the mall with four huge bags of goodies.

Jake opens the trunk and tosses the bags inside, and I stop breathing.

***

Cole

Cole pours himself a cup of coffee and takes a seat next to Mark in the entertainment room. They'd decided to play poker earlier in the evening, since Dell and Davie are starting on the night shift and wanted to join in on the fun.

"Coffee?" Mark asks, pointing a finger at Cole's mug.

Cole rubs his fingers through his hair. "No sleep for me. I have to work after this."

"You work too much," Paul says, puffing on a cigar. "You should be joining in the fun."

Mark holds up two fingers to John as he ditches two cards and picks up the new ones. "He used to have fun." Mark gives a laugh. "Seems to me the house has been pretty quiet since a little firecracker isn't around to get into trouble anymore."

"Yeah, like playing paintball or sparring in the ring," Paul adds, glancing at Cole. "Feel free to bring her back, Logan. It's getting a little dull here."

Cole rolls his eyes with a smirk. "Have you met that woman?"

"Yes," his father says, entering the room, "and we want her back."

Mark leans over the table. "Even if you can see her whenever you want, you shouldn't say that. We miss her, and what's with that bar? Have you met that creep? Mr. Scotch Neat? The man is an ass!"

"All right, boys." Abigail sets a bowl of chips and hot wings on the table. Everyone stops talking immediately as they dive in.

"Fold." Dell chucks his cards in front of him. It's their third round, and Mark has won twice, and now he's gloating.

"John, I see you and raise you five." Mark grins and turns his attention to Daniel, who looks like he's thinking.

Cole's pocket starts to vibrate. He pulls out his cell and glances at the screen, then quickly answers it. "Savi?"

"Ahh, hi. This is Jake, actually. I work with Savi at the bar." Cole looks at Mark, who's watching him. The table grows quiet. "I'm sorry for calling you, but I think she's having a panic attack or something. Any suggestions on what I should do?"

"Hold the phone up to her ear." Cole quickly walks out of the room and up the stairs, grabbing his jacket and keys.

"Okay…ahh…here she is."

Her erratic breathing fills the phone. "Savannah, it's Cole. Can you tell me what's going on?"

"I-don't—" She pauses, trying to catch a breath. "I-can't…"

"It's all right. Where are you?" he says calmly.

"M-mall." She starts to cry, her sounds muffled by the phone, then Jake is back on.

"We're at the mall parking lot, section 3C. Are you coming?"

"Yes, I'll be there in twenty."

Cole pulls into the parking lot fifteen minutes later, easily spotting Jake. Savannah is on the ground in a ball, leaning against a light pole. It's just getting dark and the temperature has dropped drastically in a very short time. He hops out and leaves the car running.

"She won't get in the car!" Jake calls out as he gets closer. "She won't come near it. I don't know what happened. One minute we were having a great time, the next she's freaking out."

Cole bends down close to Savannah. "Hey, baby, I'm going to pick you up and put you in my car now. I'll take you back to your place." She lifts her head and peers up at him through blood-shot eyes, tears streaking her face, shaking uncontrollably. She leans forward and wraps her arms around his neck.

"Cole," she whispers, sounding relieved.

He lifts her up and carries her to the car, telling Jake to follow them back home.

A few minutes later, Jake opens the door to her apartment. "I'll get changed and come back to check on her."

"It's all right, I'm going to spend the night," Cole says as he places Savannah on the couch and removes her jacket. "I called Zack. Both of your shifts are covered tonight." He stands, sighing. "Thanks for calling me, Jake. I...we...both appreciate it."

Jake hesitates, then glances at Savi, who seems to be slowly coming around. "Are you all right?"

Cole knows Jake is just looking out for her, and he respects that, but he needs to leave now. "I've got it."

"It's okay, Jake, thank you." She stands, wavering a bit. She sends him a small smile to reassure him. "I'll call you tomorrow."

Jake nods, closing the door behind him. Cole

removes his wet boots and jacket, taking in Savannah's new place. He doesn't miss the makeshift bed on the couch or the box of tissues next to it. He bends down and picks up the little army bear that had fallen on the floor, tucking it under the covers and feeling his stomach twist a little. Following the sound of the water running in the bathroom, he pushes open the door to find Savannah scrunched down in the steaming tub. Her hair is pulled up into a messy bun with a few pieces framing her face. Eyes tightly closed, she leans her head back and takes a shaky breath. Cole leans against the counter, legs and arms crossed, and watches her pale face slowly returning to its normal color.

"So what happened, Savi?" His voice is low.

She keeps her eyes closed as she speaks. "Thank you for coming and bringing me home, Cole, but you don't have to stay."

"I want to stay. Now what happened back at the mall?"

Her chin starts to quiver, and he can't help moving to her side, needing to touch her. He bends down behind her head and starts gently massaging her shoulders. The moment his hands slide over her smooth skin, he feels the mood shift. Leaning forward so his lips hover above her ear, he whispers again, "Savi, tell me what happened back there. Please talk to me, baby." He wants so much to tell her how he really feels and what he would like to do to her right now, but is afraid of her pulling back from him even more. He doesn't want her to think it's all sex between them; he loves her so much more than that. How can he explain to her that she means more to him than anything on earth? He can feel her heart beating under his hands and realizes she is holding her breath.

Suddenly she moves forward, reaching for the plug, then steps out and wraps a towel around herself. He follows her out to the living room where she hands him his jacket, not making eye contact.

"Are you kicking me out?" he asks, not taking his jacket.

"Like I said, thank you for helping me, but you can go now. I'm sure you have lots to do." She reaches to unlock the door, but he stops her. "Cole, please."

"Please what?" His hand slides down the door, meeting hers. Her hand shoots to her towel, holding it tighter around her front. "Please leave so you can crawl onto the couch and not sleep another night? Have you slept at all since Keith got switched to night duty?" She sneaks a glance at her couch. "I hate that you won't look at me." Her eyes slowly travel up his body, leaving a hot trail until they meet his. "Don't shut me out. I won't let you."

"I'm not!" she snaps, suddenly fuming with anger.

"Don't lie to me, Savi!" he snaps back.

"I'm n—"

He takes a step toward her and wraps both hands around her face. He slams his lips into hers, not caring about holding back. She pushes him away but squeaks when one hand moves the towel open and slides down her stomach and between her legs. Just as he suspected, she's ready. No matter what's going on between them, they can never deny their sexual attraction for one another.

Her hands fly out, undoing his belt and tugging down his pants, and all the while his tongue is showing her what he wants to be doing. He backs her into the kitchen as he kicks away his pants and loses his shirt. She stiffens when he lowers her down on the cold countertop and slips two fingers into her. She grabs for his erection and runs her small hands around, matching what his fingers are doing to her.

"I need to be in you," he whispers into her lips, not caring how desperate it sounds. It's the truth. She spreads her legs further as she guides him in. He sucks in a sharp breath as he tries to remember to stand. Once he's fully in, he still holds her around her waist with one hand while running his other fingertips along her slender neck, tipping her up to look at him. He leans down and brushes his lips over hers. They both have so much to say, but can't seem to find the words.

"Lean back," he orders. She complies, holding his gaze as she does so. He grips her thighs and brings her closer to the edge of the counter. His eyes rake over her body, seeing just how perfect it is. The color of her skin looks like honey, her dark hair swirling around her sexy face. The best part of this angle is her eyes. They drag him into the hot, dark pools that seem to deepen in color when he's near. He flicks forward and he rotates his hips, and her lips part as she lets out a mute moan. He starts out slowly, watching her shoot up the counter as her full breasts bounce. She arches her back to get him deeper, and he changes his grip from her thighs to her hips, rocking a little harder. His eyes shut as she squeezes him from the inside. "Damn, Savi," he groans, getting lost in the feeling. Her leg muscles tighten, and her stomach flexes as her grip on his wrists becomes rough. She's close, and so is he, but he intends to make this last for as long as he can.

He pulls out, ignoring her curses as he hauls her off the counter and over to the couch where he bends her over the arm and takes her from behind. He covers her body with his, wanting every inch of her against him. Burying her head into the covers letting out a wild scream, she orgasms under him. He didn't want to, but the intensity of her orgasm makes him go off too.

Fucking perfect.

Once he can see straight, he pulls out and scoops her up and carries her limp body into the bedroom, not bothering to turn on any lights. The moon is enough. His erection still obvious in the dim light, she spreads her legs for him, and he settles between them, pressing in gently. Those gorgeous eyes roll back in her head as he slowly slides around in the slippery mixture. Nothing in the world feels as good as being inside this woman. They spend the next few hours making love, both giving in to their desires.

They are both hot and sticky when they finally pry apart long enough to make it to the shower. By one a.m. she is curled into his chest in the bed with his fingers running up and down the length of her arm. They're totally relaxed in the blankets he had grabbed from the couch while she was drying off.

They haven't spoken much, but he needs to know what happened today.

"Savi?" he whispers, seeing if she's awake.

She shifts and moves her head slightly. "It was the trunk, in the parking lot, and," her voice is low, "it just brought me back to that day. I don't know why or what came over me, but—" He leans down and kisses her head. "Cole?"

"Mmm?"

She clears her throat, swallowing loudly. "Spend the night with me."

He smiles and turns her on her side, spooning her from behind. "Sleep, baby, I've got you."

Reaching for his hand and giving it a light kiss, she allows herself to fall asleep.

***

Savannah

I wake to Cole's arms wrapped around me tightly. I want to stay like this forever, but my bladder has a mind of its own. I wiggle out of his warm hold and move quickly to do my business, but return to find him getting dressed. I try not to show my disappointment. Now that the sun has risen, I know we're going to have to talk, so I slip on a robe and head to the kitchen, turning on the coffee maker and pulling out the cream. I turn to see Cole coming out of my room. I realize that although it feels weird seeing him here at my place, I like it. It's a step forward.

"I'm sorry, I have to get going. I have a meeting

with Frank." He moves in front of me and kisses my lips gently, then pulls away with his eyes squeezed shut like he's got something to say. "Come home with me, Savi. You don't need to prove anything to anyone."

My head snaps back and I see red instantly. "Prove anything? Cole, this isn't about anyone else. This is about me."

"If you were home, I could protect you better."

"I don't need you to protect me, I—"

"Oh, really?" His hands fly in the air. "What was that last night?"

My mouth drops open. I can't believe he's is throwing that in my face. "I didn't call you, Cole. Jake did!"

"Thank Christ he did! You were huddled in a ball in the middle of a freezing parking lot, and you wouldn't get in the car. I had to come all the way from the house to get there!" He's almost shouting. "Just come home and make it easier on everybody. You're not ready."

My blood is boiling! Why can't he see the progress I'm making? "So sorry, Cole, that I interrupted your evening. I didn't know Jake called you until he handed me the phone." I reach for my bag and pull out my phone, scrolling through my contacts until I find Sue's number and scribble it on a Post-it.

"What are you doing?" His voice is a low rumble.

I walk to the door and hold it open. "You should go." He grabs his jacket and steps out in the hallway. "Please thank your mother for the phone, but I will not be needing Shadows to care for me anymore." His face drops as I shove the cell in his hand. "I apologize for the inconvenience I caused you yesterday. Rest assured, it won't happen again." I don't wait for his response as I close the door in his face. He says something I can't make out, but I wait until I hear footsteps before I sneak a peek through the peephole. I watch as he leaves through the stairwell. My heart hurts, but I push aside the pain. I will not let my emotions run me, even if I did just let the love of my life walk out the door. *No, Savi, you kicked your love in the ass out the damn door. Fuck.*

***

I toss the rag I was using aside and jump up on the bar top. My feet are killing me. My bed is screaming—no, my couch is screaming my name. It's been nine days since I've heard from Cole. I won't lie, it hurts like hell, but I won't back down on living my life. It's painful, but I know I need this time for me. I need to be whole. Keith has even backed off. With my new phone, I texted Sue my number. I couldn't possibly freeze everyone out, especially Sue. She was there for me when I lost our baby, and I love her like my own mother. She was concerned about me, but she didn't pry.

"Can I ask you a huge favor?" Jake breaks into my thoughts, giving me the sweetest look and batting his lashes like a pro.

Oh no...

"Depends," I counter, taking the glass of wine he

just poured for me. Zack lets us drink on the house, most likely because he knows we aren't big drinkers.

"This guy I'm seeing is coming to town. It's been two months since I've seen him, and we want to go out…but his buddy is traveling with him, and he doesn't want to ditch him. Problem is—"

"He's straight, I'm straight, and I'm the only one who knows we have a—"

"Secret for a secret." He grins, knowing he's got me.

I roll my eyes and wish the internet didn't exist yet. Then my past wouldn't have come back to bite me in the ass. "When and where?"

"Yay!" He claps then looks around quickly as he realizes we are still at work.

"Okay, Jake, as long as he knows he's not getting laid and there's zero chance of a second date."

"Of course." He jumps off the counter. "Thursday, drinks at Chaps."

"What the hell is Chaps?" I call out.

He turns and gives me a devilish grin. "We live in Montana, sweetheart."

I close my eyes, thinking a shopping trip may be in order…cowgirl boots are something I don't own.

***

Cole

Cole: Where?

Keith: Still at work, having a drink with Jake.

Cole: Let her know.

Keith: Will do.

Cole makes his way into the living room where Abigail is nursing a cup of tea. She's been battling a nasty cold and hasn't been able to sleep very well.

She gives him a warm smile. "Come sit with me, honey." She pats the seat next to her, and he does without a second thought. "You look stressed. Tell Aunt Abby what's going on in that handsome head of yours."

He smiles at the words she has used for as long as he can remember. "I think I may have pushed when I shouldn't have," he admits, letting out a long sigh. "We spent the night together, and in the morning, I pushed too hard, saying she should come back." He shrugs, feeling lost. "I know I made it seem like it would be easier for everyone if she did, and I wasn't thinking about how much she's accomplished since she left. Savi kicked me out, Abigail, and gave me back the phone with all of our contacts in it."

"Well, that explains the radio silence." Abigail sips her tea.

He runs his hand along his neck. "She's so stubborn, and I love that, but…" He can't finish the sentence.

"What if she moves on to someone else?" she asks, finishing his question. He nods, as a shot to his stomach has him in discomfort. "Cole, you know Savannah only has eyes for you, but she needs some time to breathe without someone dictating her every move. Let her walk a little on her own, then she'll run back to you. I promise."

"How do you know?"

She sits her tea cup on her saucer and takes his hand in hers. "Because I've been on this earth a lot longer than you, and I know true love when I see it. You're lucky enough to have found it this early in life. Most of us wait a lifetime or never find it. Give her space, honey. She loves you. Never doubt that."

"All right." He leans back and lets out a long sigh and watches the fire, trying to convince himself that Abby knows best. She usually does.

***

Savannah

I open my door to find Keith sitting on my couch and staring at his phone, and it makes the hair stand up on the back of my neck. He stands, and I know something isn't right.

"Sit, Savi." He nods to the chair, and I do. "You leave tomorrow morning for Washington. Pack enough for three days, and I'll pick you up at seven a.m." He heads for the door. "I'll see you then."

"Umm, okay," I whisper, feeling the layer of ice that has formed over our friendship.

He starts to leave, but stops. "How are you doing?"

"I'm fine," I lie, reluctant to draw on my earlier fight with Cole. He closes the door behind him, leaving me reeling with the thought of seeing The American again.

Sleep doesn't happen, if it ever even was a possibility. I'm running on thirty minutes per night. Once Jake spent the night after drinking too much, and I managed to get in a solid four hours. It's just not the same as being wrapped in Cole's safety net.

At six I'm packed and out the door, tired of staring at the living room wall. Yes, my place seems homier since Jake helped me decorate, but one could go crazy with how much I'm staring at it. I slip a note under Jake's door letting him know I'll be gone for a few days and to help himself to my coffee. We exchanged keys a few days ago.

I take the elevator because I have time and find myself a chair in the lobby. The man behind the desk gives me a nod before going back to playing something on his phone. I count how many times the heater kicks in, how many tiles are on the floor and ceiling, and how many times the man at the desk glances my way. After sitting for forty-five minutes, I can't take any more. Needing to do something, I open my phone to the only two numbers saved, Jake and Sue, and press call on the second name.

"Savannah?" Sue asks, puzzled. She has a right to be. I haven't spoken to her in over a week, and no doubt she's heard about my blow-up with Cole. I'm not trying to be distant with her; I just find it easier to pull away from everyone at the house altogether.

"Hi, Sue. Did I wake you?"

She gives a little laugh. "No, I've been up for some time. You know how I love the mornings."

She pauses. "Is everything all right, dear?"

No. "Yes, I'm…" *Lost, tired, scared about my trip.* "I just wanted to see how you are."

"I'm fine. I've just been battling the snow like everyone this winter. How are you holding up?"

"Fine," I answer too quickly.

I hear her seat creak. "Okay, so we played the pleasant, do you want to tell me why you're really calling?"

"I'm scared," I confess.

"About? Your trip?"

I close my eyes. Of course she knows about Washington. "Yes, and then some."

"The trip, I understand. I would be too. That's perfectly normal." She pauses. "What else are you afraid of, Savannah?"

I reach for my necklace and clasp the snowflake pendant. My throat tightens with thoughts of Cole, but no words come out because I don't even know where to start.

"Savi, when you get back, I want you to come to Shadows and spend Saturday afternoon and evening with us. It's been too long since you've been home, and everyone misses you. I understand you need your space, but it's not healthy for you to isolate yourself from everyone who loves you." *Home.* The word drips with emotion. I miss everyone terribly. How can I say no to Sue?

"All right," I whisper in fear my voice will break. I look up and see Keith speaking with the security guard. He's eyeing me as I say goodbye to Sue.

Chapter Three

"You ready?" Keith asks, reaching for the handle of my suitcase. I follow him out into the morning frost. It's still dark, making everything seem that much colder. The SUV is still warm, and we drive in silence all the way to the airport. It saddens me that Keith is pulling away, but can I blame him? It's what I told Cole I needed. Isn't it what I want, the chance to find myself? I can't do it if I have Keith taking care of me every day. So I keep my mouth shut, face forward, and try to push back the sneaking fear that's dancing along my spine.

The airport is quiet, with hardly anyone around. Keith hands me my ticket as someone approaches us. I watch as Keith holds out his hand and gives the man a firm handshake.

"Savannah, this is Agent Hahn. He's on Frank's detail. He'll be traveling with you to Washington and making sure you are well briefed before the testimony." I nearly fall over right there. Keith isn't coming; he won't be my rock as I go through all of this. "You'll be fine, and I'll be here to pick you up when you return." My heart slams into my stomach, looking for a way out.

I'm mute. All I can do is give a slight nod and follow Agent Hahn to the gate, where we walk out to the tiny plane and board. The plane that will drop me off at the feet of my worst nightmare.

As soon as we are in the air, I mentally check out.

***

Cole

Cole listens to his father brief him and his team about a target who needs to be extracted from Mexico City. They are possibly holding a child for ransom, and the parents happen to be the owner of the Garrisons' Casinos, one of the biggest casino companies worldwide and known to have a shady side. They've been asked to check it out and see what they can come up with.

Keith knocks and steps inside the door, halting the conversation. "Savi is on the plane. She should be there within the hour."

Mark's jaw drops as he shifts in his seat. "You didn't go with her?" Keith shakes his head, and Mark turns to look at Cole. "Why didn't he go?"

"We have to work," Cole mutters, picking up a file, but apparently Mark has more to say.

"Ummm, what?" Mark pushes himself out of his chair and stares at them. "You mean Savi is on that plane by herself?"

"Let it go," Daniel warns.

"No! Someone should be with her. She's facing The American and Lynn! Cole, you should be there, not hiding behind your desk."

Cole drops the thick folder, making John jump. "You don't think I want to be there, Mark? You don't think it's turning me inside out that my girl is a state away and only an arm's length from the people who tried to kill her? I was *ordered* to stay behind and do my job. I was *ordered* to leave for Mexico when all I want to do is be in that courtroom with her. I'm not hiding. I'm following orders since I didn't last time. I *have* to, for the sake of everyone, especially for the sake of Shadows' reputation." His anger is seeping out of him as he looks at Mark, who has backed off and is nodding. He gets it now.

Paul's phone rings, taking some of the tension from the room. "We have a hit. We should get moving."

***

Savannah

I shake the entire drive to the Washington base. Agent Hahn is friendly, but I just want to stay in my zone, turned off, not answering questions about the weather. We really have nothing in common. I think of Sue, wondering if I should call her just to hear her voice…but that's not the voice I really want to hear.

"Hello again, Savannah." Frank smiles as he greets me at the car. "Please come inside." He hands me a visitor badge and leads me into a large gray building where everything is muted, from the color of the walls to the people's clothing and even their voices. "This is my office. Can I get you anything?"

"Coffee would be great, thanks," I say in a quiet voice to fit the surroundings, then take a seat across from his dull metal desk littered with papers. On the wall are a few pictures of a younger version of Frank starting out in the Army, and two others with President Obama and former President Bush. Medals hang in wooden boxes, and an old-fashioned rifle sits in the corner as though waiting to be mounted. He probably never got around to doing it. He hands me a coffee before he takes a seat. "Thank you."

Flipping open a file, he gets right to it. "So you were first taken from your condo in New York by a Raul Paru."

"Please jump right in," I mutter, taken aback. "I don't know who Raul Paru even is." Frank hands me a picture, and it takes me a minute, but then I see it, and the memory comes flooding back. My cut leg, the cold, thick substance which later I found out was blood, and the smell in the van. "The painters? These guys were painting my condo the week I was taken. I remember his belt buckle," I say as I press my finger against the buckle in the photo. I'll never forget that longhorn Texas belt buckle.

"Yes, they were scoping out the place, watching you, learning your habits."

I hand the picture back and remember Lynn making a comment about how you can buy those belt buckles on any street corner. I feel the wind being sucked out of me. That bitch! I can't believe she knew what they were doing because she fucking hired them! I wonder how many other times I ran into people she had hired to help take me out.

Frank and I go over all the details of my file, and I am pretty much fried by the time I am taken back to my hotel by Agent Hahn, who is staying with me. I am thankful for the two bedroom suite. He offers to order dinner for both of us, but I decline, just wanting to get some sleep. Tomorrow Frank has me meeting some lawyers, and I want to be able to stay awake for all the legal talk that's to come.

***

The day is a blur much like the first. I am taken into a conference room and questioned for about four hours on practically the same things, only worded differently. They give me so much advice I almost forget my own name. I'm not sure if I am coming or going. Finally, after I am about to throw in the towel, they inform me that I am to wear a simple black dress with heels, and wear my hair down with no jewelry. I reach for my chain and hold it tightly, and one of the women agrees it is fine, but nothing more. They don't want me looking too flashy. I don't understand why, but I'm beyond caring. I just need to get through tomorrow, and then I can get back to my mountain.

"You want something to eat?" Agent Hahn asks as we walk back to the hotel. I shake my head. "How about a drink?" I look up to see him smiling.

"I could really use a drink after that."

"That sounds really good, actually." I smile back and follow him to a small Mexican restaurant.

"Umm," I point to the sign, "not to be a pain, but can we get anything else but Mexican food?"

Agent Hahn chuckles a little, then points across the street to an Italian joint. "Is that better?"

"Much, thanks." I follow him to the crosswalk. We take a seat in the corner of the restaurant and are soon sipping a glass of merlot.

"How are you holding up?" he asks, picking up a piece of bread, dipping it in some oil and vinegar, and popping in it his mouth.

I shrug because I really don't know. "Ask me tomorrow."

He chuckles but grows quiet, thinking. "Do you know who I am?"

My fingers twist the stem of the glass, making the wine run up the sides then bleed back down, leaving heavy lines. "No, but if you're about to tell me you work for The American or the Cartels at least give me a five minute head start."

"Ha!" He tosses his head back. "No, hell no. I was the one who found Logan the day he escaped."

"Oh," I whisper, instantly feeling indebted to this guy.

"I was also there when you were found at The American's house," he adds.

I smile at him. I'm starting to get used to the fact that so many people have met me at some point, even if I don't remember them. I feel the need to explain my behavior. "I'm sorry I've been so standoffish. I'm just trying to get through this so I can figure out what I want to do with what's left of my life."

"Sounds exhausting."

"It is!" I laugh, thinking it's nice to still be able to.

Our food comes, and we pick away, talking about little things. It isn't until he brings up the training for the Green Berets that something nags at me from the edge of my memory *again.*

"What?" he asks, seeing my face.

"Ever have this feeling you're forgetting something important?" I close my eyes and try to think. "I think it's got something to do with Davie...the newest recruit at the house." I see Agent Hahn studying me. "I'm sorry, it's nothing."

"It's okay. Yes, I have, and it's annoying."

"Very," I agree. "It's like seeing the end of a rope, but it's just out of reach, I feel like if I could only grab it and tug, the memory would come to me." I laugh and shake my head. "Oh well, tomorrow is going to be exhausting. I guess we should get back."

"Yeah," he grabs his coat, "let's get back."

"Agent Hahn?"

"Yes?" He turns to look at me.

"Thanks for taking me out for dinner and the talk. It helped a bit."

He hands me my hat. "Happy to hear that, Savannah."

Later, lying in bed with a slight buzz on, just enough to keep the shakes away, but not enough to make my head stop spinning thinking about tomorrow, my cellphone goes off beside me. A flutter of hope that maybe it's Cole goes through me, but it's not.

Jake: Coffee doesn't taste right.

I smirk and roll onto my side.

Savi: Yes it does.

Jake: It does, but I'm bored without you.

I miss my friend too.

Savi: Sorry. I'm coming home Thursday morning.

Jake: Good! You still on for our double date?

Shit.

Savi: It's not a date, but yes.

Jake: You want some dirt? I have good and bad.

I think for a moment…

Savi: Maybe…bad first?

There's a small pause, and I wonder if the news is about work. I wonder if someone got fired. Yikes, I hope not.

Jake: I saw Logan in town yesterday…with the town bitch Christina. She had her claws all over him. Just thought you should know.

My stomach sinks…oh…

Jake: Now for the good news! Zack hired some new staff…we're talking yummy staff! I think one may play for my team. One can dream.

I flop on my back and feel my heart squeeze to the point of pain.

Savi: Thanks for letting me know, and I hope so for your sake.

Jake: You all right?

Not at all.

Savi: I hope after tomorrow. I should go…night.

Jake: Call me if you need to chat. Night, Savi. xo

***

"You look…"

"I know." I snag the coffee Hahn got me and take a few long sips. "I didn't get much sleep."

"Did you get any?" he asks, slipping into his suit jacket and taking in the dark circles under my eyes.

"Would you?"

"No, probably not." He checks the time. "We should go."

Frank works wonders with this case, keeping the media at bay. The only ones who know I am going to be in court today are the lawyers and the judge.

I am told to sit on a bench and wait for my name to be called. Agent Hahn and Frank are busy talking to the lawyers down the hall, far enough away that I can't hear what they're saying.

My nerves are shot. I can feel a slight trembling starting in my legs. To say I'm scared would be putting it mildly. I am freaking out, full throttle. Every breath I take gets harder, like there is a weight on my chest. My phone goes off, making my purse vibrate. I was supposed to turn it off, but I forgot. Not thinking, I answer it.

"Hello?"

"Savannah?" Cole's voice washes over me. "Are you all right? Are you at the court?"

"I-I don't think I can do this." The words slip past my lips. "I don't want to do this."

"Hey, baby, you can. Think about how much your testimony will count. How long he will go away for. I know this is scary, but you are strong, and you can do this."

I hold on to his words, wishing so much he was here with me. Just hearing his voice helps to steady me.

"Savannah Miller," a clerk calls out. Agent Hahn and Frank come toward me, and I feel panic setting in.

"Cole! I…I have to go."

"Savi—"

"Thanks for the call." I hang up and turn my phone off. I can't listen to what he has to say. It might break the last straw holding me up.

The clerk holds open the door as I step into the massive courtroom. Surprisingly, there aren't that many people inside. My head stays straight as I walk past the table of lawyers whose eyes seem to be burning holes in me. My heart pounds three beats for every one step I take. I stand in front of the chair and behind the table while the officer asks me to raise my right hand and place the other on the Bible. I swallow hard, my throat dry. I'm hot. *Why is it so damn hot in here?*

I nervously take a seat as the prosecutor approaches to ask me a series of questions. Things seem to move slowly at first. I have to recall the day I was taken, then describe the events of my seven months in captivity, and finally about when I was rescued. I'm so tired, but I'm here, so I can't stop now even if I want to. I keep my gaze fixed on Frank, who nods to let me know he's with me. Then the questions start to pick up, coming at me faster and faster and not giving me a chance to think.

"You say you saw my client? But yet you said you couldn't see his face? That doesn't make any sense, Ms. Miller."

"It was him, I know—"

"How do you know? How do you know it wasn't someone else?"

"Because I know—"

The lawyer smirks at me. "You need evidence, Ms. Miller. You can't just go on a hunch." I start to speak, but he cuts me off *again.* "Now, you said my client allegedly killed Luka Donovan. Are you sure, or is this just another hunch?"

"I saw him pull the trigger," I say, and can't hold back a snicker. I see Frank shake his head, warning me to calm down.

The lawyer picks up a small remote and points it at a screen. "Ms. Miller, you have a reputation for getting the attention of the media, yes?" My blood boils, but he doesn't wait for me to answer before a picture of me comes up on the screen. I gasp at the intoxicated picture of me published in US Weekly. He flips through several, and some I hadn't even seen before. "I'd say the camera loves you." His voice positively drips with sarcasm. "You never liked that your father was in politics, did you? And you obviously intended to make it a rough climb for him."

"Objection, Your Honor, badgering the witness."

"Sustained. Mr. Wilson, please get on with it."

The lawyer holds a hand over his chest. "Of course, Your Honor." He turns back to me. "You got yourself into trouble with the media quite a bit, yes?"

"No, that's not what—"

"So you used the media as your outlet, smearing the papers with the fact that he has a drunk for a daughter."

"Objection!" my lawyer calls out.

"Withdrawn, Your Honor." The sleazy lawyer puts his hands in the air.

What the hell?

Withdrawn or not, the twelve jurors still heard

that lie. He faces me again. "You have to admit the media was only too willing to jump at a chance to print pictures of you."

He turns to the jurors and points a finger in my direction. "I think Ms. Miller was looking for a way to get back at her father for going into politics when he should have been at home helping her care for her sick mother. So she made a plan with Deputy Mayor Luka Donovan," my mouth drops open at this ridiculously untrue comment, "a plan that she would be kidnapped with the help of her best friend Lynn, who has had a small taste of political life and wants more. So much more that she seeks help from an old friend who happens to be Raul Paru, a known drug carrier for the Mexican Cartel. Ms. Miller gets 'taken' and stays in Cabo for several months until the U.S. Army gets involved and things get messy. So Raul Paru gets spooked and decides to set up his brother-in-law." The lawyer points to his client, who I can't look at. "My client, Denton Barlow." The jury looks at me, confused, like they're trying to piece this new information together. "Ms. Miller seduced, used, and manipulated my client into thinking she loved him. She even went so far as to sleep with him. She used him for sex, information, money—"

That's it! I hit my breaking point. I can't take these lies any longer!

I jump to my feet with tears streaming down my face. "I was taken from my home in the middle of the night!" I scream, making everyone jump. "I was treated like a filthy animal, fed scraps, dirty water, bug infested bread. Beaten till I couldn't feel the pain anymore, for seven goddamn months!" I point at The American, looking him straight in the eye for the first time. "You bought me like a piece of meat. You said you loved me, and I despised you. I wasn't like the other women who believed your words. I am strong enough to see you for what you are, weak!" The judge is yelling something, but I'm not listening. As far as I'm concerned, it is just me and The American in this courtroom, and for once he can't touch me. "I know the truth, Denton, no matter what happens here today. I know you're a coward, that you buy women because they can't love the real you, they *can't stand* the real you. Rot in hell, you sick son of a bitch." My arm is being tugged as an officer hauls me out of the courtroom. I'm pressed into Frank's hold and taken into a small room.

"Jesus Christ, Savannah!" Frank says, running a hand over his buzz cut.

I lean over the table, suddenly exhausted. "I want to go home," I whisper.

"Savannah, you still need to testify against Lynn."

I can't. I won't. I'm finished. "No." I stand straight and my head spins. "I'm done, Frank." I open the door and walk out.

***

Cole

Cole holds the little boy's body close to his chest as they step off the chopper and head toward the safe house. Poor little guy passed out during the rescue operation. The kidnappers had Ryder for six days, tied to a bed in an old warehouse. All things considered, he's all right. Abigail comes rushing up and takes Ryder from Cole, whisking him inside to a warm bed. His aunt is cleared to take him into a witness protection program tomorrow. For now, the little guy just needs rest.

During Cole's much-anticipated hot shower, he hears his phone ringing next to the sink. He clears the glass on the door and sees it's Frank. He reaches out and answers it.

"Frank, what's going on?"

"Oh, fuck, they were rough on her." Frank's voice is bone tired "They called her every name in the book, saying she was the mastermind, that she seduced Denton. It was nasty."

Shit.

"How is she?"

There's a pause. "She lost it at one point and yelled at Denton, until she got kicked out."

"Fuck." Cole leans his head against the wet glass.

"Yeah, well, she left saying she was done. We lost her, her phone is off, and the hotel room is empty. So I'm guessing she's heading home."

Cole turns the water off. "All right, I'll figure it out. Just deal with the shit on your end."

By the time Cole starts downstairs, Keith is heading up. "She arrived at the airport. She's in a cab heading back to her place. I'd have offered to go get her, but she didn't call me. She called your mother."

Cole nods and pulls out his phone, but Keith stops him. “I don’t care if she needs space, I’m not staying away. She’s family, and if she’s hurting—”

“I know, and I agree.” Cole sighs and brings the phone to his ear. His mother answers.

“Cole, she’s all right,” his mother says calmly. “I just left her place, and Jake said he’ll take her out to get something to eat. She’s upset, but she’s holding it together for now.”

“All right. Thanks, Mom.”

“Anytime, honey.”

After getting absolutely nothing productive done at work, Cole decides to check in on Ryder, who is still fast asleep in Savannah’s old room. “Looks so small,” he says softly to Abigail, who is sitting quietly beside the bed.

“It’s truly sad that anyone should be kidnapped, but a five year old child?” Abigail presses a hand against her chest. “Poor little angel must have been so scared.”

“Savages,” Cole mutters and checks the time. Seven thirty. “I need to go out. Call me if he wakes.”

“Of course.” She smiles slightly. “Tell Savannah I say hello.”

A short time later, Cole knocks on Savannah’s apartment door, but there’s no answer, and no answer at Jake’s either, so he heads down to speak with the security guard.

“She left about an hour and a half ago looking mighty pretty. She was with her neighbor. Think they said something about Chaps bar.”

Why would she go to Chaps to eat?

"Thanks."

Cole heads back out into the cold air, wondering what the hell is going on. Is that why she didn't want Keith coming to get her, because she had plans to go to a bar tonight? This doesn't sound like Savi.

Chaps is loud and crowded. Every type of cowboy boot and hat known to man is in this bar tonight. He feels very out of place; this is *not* his scene. Nor did he think it was Savannah's. He uses his weight to move through thc sea of bodies, pulling down his black baseball cap to shade his eyes from the blinding lights as he scans the faces. He soon spots Jake and heads over.

"Where is she?" Cole shouts over *Big and Rich.*

Jake sighs, shaking his head at his friend. "Look, Logan, she's out on a date. She's had a horrible day and needs a night off."

Feeling like he just got sucker punched in the gut, Cole sees red. "Where is she, Jake?"

Jake rubs his face, then decides to make the right choice.

"Bruno's Cheesecake. Please let her enjoy her evening. She's in rough shape." Cole doesn't respond as he charges back outside.

Watching her through the cafe window, Cole sees she's in a tight pair of skinny jeans and a black lace tank top, wearing red cowboy boots. Her hair is in big curls tumbling down her back, and silver earrings sparkle as she shakes her head, smiling at the man across the table from her, who looks very interested in *his* Savannah.

He lets out a heavy puff of air and leans back so she doesn't see him. He takes out his phone and allows his thumb to rub over the screen. His hand twitches with the need to call her. A movement draws his attention back to her. Her date is standing, says something, then walks off, probably to order a drink. Turning her face toward the window, he sees her expression fall like she is about to cry. She pulls out her cell phone, checks the screen, and looks disappointed. *Maybe*? A tap on his back makes him jump and almost drop his phone. "What the hell!" Mark is standing behind him with a huge grin on his face.

"Whatcha doin'?"

Cole can't help but grin back; they are both spying on her. "How's her night going?"

Mark leans to peek in the window. "She started out at Chaps, but she didn't hang in there for long. She wasn't diggin' it. On the walk back, buddy tried to hold her hand, but she wouldn't let him. They've been here for about an hour. He's interested but respectful, so we'll see how the rest of the night goes." Cole glances over at her and sees her smile, but it's not touching her eyes. "She seems sad tonight. I heard the lawyer did a number on her." Mark clears his throat. "I think it would be good if she saw you tonight, Cole. Seriously, she's hurting."

"I don't know," Cole sighs, not knowing what to do.

"Fine, I'll make the decision for you. I could be out here freezing my ass off, or I could be in bed with Mel." He shrugs. "So, goodnight!" With that, he jogs away, laughing.

Fuck.

After climbing back into his SUV, he turns the heat up and hunkers down for a long night. Twenty-five minutes later, they're up and leaving Bruno's and heading down toward her apartment. He starts the engine and creeps down the street, parking a few spots away. She stops at the door and says goodbye, and the guy smiles and reaches for her hips, pulling her into him. She shakes her head as he goes in for a kiss, but he's too quick and misses her signals, planting a kiss on her lips. Fire burns through Cole's veins and his hand flies to the door handle, but he quickly stops himself as he takes in her reaction. She raises her hands and pushes him away, saying no. The guy steps back immediately, obviously apologizing, and hands her something that looks like a card. She takes it, waving him goodbye, then waits for him to walk away before she disappears inside, leaving Cole more than a little relieved, but also feeling pretty shitty for spying.

Chapter Four

Savannah

I work my shift like a robot, not speaking any more than I have to. Jake is the polar opposite, and is chatting on and on, excited about Graham, the new member of the wait staff. Graham resembles Taylor Lautner, no joke. I keep waiting for him to bust into a werewolf. My mind is spinning with thoughts of going to the safe house tomorrow. I truly hope no one wants to talk about what happened in Washington. Frank called this morning and informed me I'm being ordered back to testify against Lynn. It's out of his control, and he felt terrible for what happened with Denton's lawyer.

Jake suddenly grabs my hands and shakes me. "Why are you so distant? I need my wingman!"

I push all my crap aside and try to be a better friend. "How do you even know he's gay?"

"That's what I need you for." I raise an eyebrow, not sure I'm going to like this plan. "When he comes over here next time, lean over the bar to grab his order slip, then pretend to drop it and give him an ass view."

Oh Lord.

"What if he doesn't look, gets distracted or something?"

He gives me a don't-be-stupid look. "If he's straight, he won't be looking anywhere else."

Seeing someone snag a seat, I turn to focus on him, and realizing who it is, I smile and bend down to take his order.

Davie leans over so I can hear him over the crowd. "I heard you were working here. We have the night off, and I thought we should stop in and say hello."

"Well, thanks. What can I get you and…?"

"Two Fat Tires, and it's Dell. The rest of the guys are at some place down the street."

I pour his drinks, take a few more orders, and wait for the dinner rush to slow down a little. We normally have a slow dip at seven. Dell joins Davie, drinking a few beers. I try to engage them as best as I can, but Don, the woman repeller, is back, and apparently it's his last night before he returns to wherever the hell the devil spat him out from.

"Savi!" Jake whispers, nodding his head toward Graham, who is heading our way. "You're up!"

I roll my eyes and do as I was asked. I smile, lean in, grab the slip, drop it, and bend over. I make his order and fill my tray.

"Thanks, Savi." Graham smiles.

"Sure thing, Taylor," I joke back, but burst out laughing when he lets out a howl. Okay, so he's been called that before.

"Heard it all before." His gaze goes from joking to smirking as Jake appears at my side. "Nice performance, Savi, but I play for both teams." He winks and walks away, and my jaw drops as Jake puts his head to my shoulder in a fit of laughter.

"Oh my god!" I hit Jake's arm. "You're welcome."

"Does anyone actually work here?" I hear her call out from the other side of the bar. Jake mutters something as he approaches Christina, the evil bitch. "No," she flicks her finger, dismissing Jake, "her."

Oh hell, speaking of the Devil's shit…I make my way over, not missing the way Dell is scowling at her. "Three margaritas, one Stella, one glass of pino, and two shots of tequila," she barks at me. "You think you can handle that, or should I write it down?" I bite my tongue just as her friend comes up. "I was with him again last night," she says loudly enough for me to hear.

"Who?" I decide to play the game.

"Logan." She glances at me, making sure I can hear her as she turns her attention elsewhere. "He came out to the bar, then we went back to my place." She looks at her friend. "I love running my hands over his tattoo." I tune her out, mainly because Cole said he never slept with her. I hate that she can even get a rise out of me. A small niggle of doubt nestles inside me, right by my heart. I place her drinks in front of her and tell her the total. She flicks her credit card at me, hitting my arm.

Don't hit her, don't hit her.

After she signs the slip with no tip, she leans over but talks nice and loud. "If you know what's good for you, sweetheart, you'll stay away from him. He's mine, and I have ways of making people like you disappear."

I have a great comeback, I really do. I can be feisty, but the word *disappear* sends me three steps back. So instead, I change course. I wait for her to leave and pretend not to see the concern written all over Dell's face. I turn to Don and make my move. Leaning over, I whisper in his ear. He smiles and checks my cleavage once more before he grabs his drink and heads over to her table.

Davie is shaking his head when I return to watch the show. "What did you say to him?"

"Just that if he wants a farewell fuck, he's guaranteed to find it over there, because after three drinks she'll be pouring herself into his bed." I smirk and head off to take some more orders.

"It's dead," Zack announces by eleven. "Chaps is having some BOGO special, so why don't you guys go home early?" Jake and I don't move. It's sad we don't have Friday night plans. "All right, let's do one better," Zack says, shaking his head at both of us as he drops three shot glasses on the bar. He slips two straws over the hole, pouring the tequila in three different streams, filling all the glasses at once. *Impressive.* "Cheers."

I slide my butt onto the bar top and take the drink, chasing it with a lime. Graham drops off his tray on the bar and asks Jake if he knows of a place to go for a late meal. Jake smiles at me knowingly as he grabs his tips. I laugh and wave them both off.

"So, Savannah, how are you liking living in town?" Zack asks as he pours me another.

I drink it quickly. "It's nice."

Zack hops up on the other side of the bar top and turns to face me. "I know this is none of my business and a little late, but I am sorry about what happened in your life."

"Thanks." I shrug, taking a moment to think. "I think the worst part of it all is feeling like I don't really belong anywhere. I can't go back to New York for so many reasons. I have no family or friends there. I left Shadows because I felt like I needed to find myself, like they were worrying about me when they should be focusing on their open cases." I glance over at him, realizing I'm complaining. "Sorry, didn't mean to toss you into my pity party."

He shakes his head. "No, it sounds exactly like someone should in your situation. The only difference is their hearts aren't invested in someone tall, dark, and handsome." I smile and throw a sigh. He's right. "When I retired from Shadows, I couldn't leave. My family is here. What's that saying? Home is where the heart is. This is where my heart wants to be, and I lucked out that my brother came and joined me." He pours me one more, but stops me when I go to drink it. "You may not think you've settled or put down any roots, Savannah, but you have a house full of people who care about you up on that mountain, and you have two in this restaurant. Stop worrying about what you *should* be feeling and just feel. Life is too short to float, so sink a little and start living." He holds up his glass. "To you."

"To me." I raise my drink and drop it back, letting his words absorb. "Now," I clap my hands together, needing to change the subject, "I want some juicy stories on Cole and Mark when they were younger."

***

Cole

Cole hangs up the phone with Frank feeling *off* with their conversation about Ryder's parents. They owe a lot of money and are more concerned about their casino than where their child might be. Abigail said the boy isn't coming out of his room, which seems normal, but they only had one child here before, and she was a little older. This is new for everyone. He was glad Dr. Roberts would arrive around twelve to evaluate him, then Frank could take him into town where is aunt is waiting.

His phone alerts him he has a text.

Mark: Living room.

Cole makes his way down the hallway, hearing all kinds of voices. The smile on Abigail's face makes his stomach twist, then he sees her hugging June. It's been three weeks, but she's really here in his living room. Savannah sees him and gives him a little smile, one that makes him want to grab her toss her over his shoulder and take her upstairs.

"Hi." Her eyes are deep and dark. "Can we talk

when you have a moment?"

"Sure," he nods as her eyes drop to his lips momentarily. At least he sees she's still drawn to him, and his pants tighten as he breathes her in. He needs to be alone with her now. "You want to talk in my office?"

"No!" June squeals. "She just got here. You can talk about whatever later, but right now I want to hear all about what she's been up to." She grabs Savi's hand and starts pulling her to the couch. *Damn you, June...*

They talk and talk...you would think Savi has been gone for months. The only thing keeping him going is listening to her voice. God, he missed her voice, her laugh, the way she sneaks a peek at him every once in a while. Just letting him know she's thinking of him.

After some time, he heads back into his office. He has some emails to send before he can take the evening off. Now that Savannah is here, he wants to wrap this up faster.

"Cole," June whispers from his doorway. "Cole, you've got to come see this." He groans when he loses his train of thought. "It's Savi." He looks up and sees her smile now that she's got his attention. "You have to see this." He follows her out the door. "After everyone started doing their own thing and the place quieted down, Keith asked Savi to make him his favorite cookies, and," she pauses, "just look..."

He peeks around the corner, seeing Savannah in an apron, hair pulled up and speaking quietly.

"You want to crack the egg?" she asks Ryder,

who is sitting on the island helping Savannah make the cookies. He turns back to June, who's beaming.

"He came into the kitchen and took her hand. She sat on the floor and started talking to him, then asked if he wanted to make cookies, and he said yes. She even lifted him up on there. He doesn't like being touched, Cole. He doesn't really take to any of us, but he likes her." June signals her sister to come see what they're looking at.

Savannah picks up a spoon and dips it into the jar of peanut butter from when she made Ryder's sandwich earlier. "You know what I love to do when no one's looking?" Ryder shakes his head and giggles when she scoops a spoonful of peanut butter and pops the spoon in her mouth. "You want to try?" She picks up another spoon and hands it to him. He hesitates, but she encourages him to do it, and he shoves a huge glob of peanut butter into his little mouth. "Great job!" She high-fives him.

"Natural born mother." Abigail peeks up at Cole.

"What are we looking at?" Dr. Roberts whispers, making the three of them jump.

"Ryder likes Savannah," Abigail answers.

Dr. Roberts takes a peek, then steps into view. Cole moves into the kitchen too, but stays back. Ryder spots the doctor and grabs Savannah's arm. "Good afternoon, Savannah. What are you making?"

"Hello, Doc. Ryder and I are making Keith's favorite oatmeal chocolate chip cookies."

"They smell good," he says, staying a few away. He watches as Ryder buries his head into her shoulder. Her hand runs along his back, soothing him. "I was wondering if Ryder would come and draw me a picture." Ryder doesn't move, but Savi bends down to his eye level.

"You know what, Ryder? My favorite color is purple. Would you draw me a picture so I can hang it on the fridge? The boys in this house never draw me any pictures." She gives a loud sigh and smiles at him lovingly as he looks from the doctor to her again. He finally nods his little brown head and reaches out so she'll help him down.

"Let's go to the dining room, it's just right there, and draw Savannah a picture." Doc Roberts leads the way, leaving the two of them in the kitchen. Savannah goes back to making the cookies.

"That was pretty impressive," Cole says, coming to stand by the island where she's working.

She rolls some dough into a ball, dropping it on the tray. "He's a sweet little boy."

"You got him to eat. He hasn't eaten in two days."

"I know that feeling," she whispers, turning to stick the tray into the oven.

"How are things working out at Zack's?" he asks, trying to feel her out.

Davie comes in and scoops some of the cookie dough out with a spoon. "Other than the threats, I'd say she's doing pretty good," he says. Savannah glares at him, but he's too busy eating to notice.

Cole stiffens. "Threats?"

"It's nothing," she says over her shoulder.

"Nothing! That bitch has it out for you, Savi. I'd watch my back. You should have heard what her and her friends were say—"

"Davie," Savannah interrupts, "could you tell Keith the first batch is in the oven?"

"Sure." He takes another spoonful of cookie dough before he leaves.

"Who?" Cole's voice is harsh. "Don't lie, Savi."

She drops her head and sighs. "Christina." *Fuck me*. "I handled it, but if you could tell her not to threaten me at work, that would help. I don't need to hear about you two hooking up with all the customers around."

"Hooking up?" Cole moves off the stool and comes around to her side. "She said we were hooking up?"

"Yes, last night and a few other times. Whatever, just tell her to back off." She won't look at him.

"Savi, I wasn't with her last night."

"Okay," she mutters, brushing him off.

Fuck... "I was watching you, on your date." Her face snaps up. "I watched you at Bruno's, and later when he kissed you outside your apartment."

"You were spying on me?"

He shakes his head. "I was protecting what's mine."

"Oh my god!" She drops the wooden spoon she was using. "You broke up with *me,* remember, Cole. I wanted space, but I never wanted it from you." She reaches for the oven as the timer goes off. He waits until she's finished before pinning her in the corner of the counter.

"How did it feel when his lips touched yours?" He needs to know what she's really feeling right now, in this moment. His thumb runs along her bottom lip, making her mouth part. "Did you like it?

Did you like the way he tastes?" She barely shakes her head as he leans in and runs his tongue along her lower lip. She sags into him as he starts kissing her, reminding her who owns this mouth.

"Cole," she says, pulling away as he kisses her jaw, "why didn't you come to Washington? I needed you." He stops and moves to look her in the eye.

"I had orders to get Ryder from Mexico City. I crossed the line falling for you, so when they tell me to do a job, I have to do it." He cups her cheek. "I wanted to be with you so badly, I used the satellite phone to call you, and that's a big no." She closes her eyes and leans forward, resting her head against his chest. His hands rub small circles across her back. "I'll be there when you testify against Lynn."

She pulls away. "I don't want to."

"You have to, Savi."

"I…"

"Ohh, so close," Keith says to Mark behind them like they are watching a movie.

Mark scrunches his face. "Yeah, I thought Cole had her this time." He laughs with Keith, then looks at Cole and Savannah. "What? We're bored." He shrugs, not caring at all that they're intruding on a personal moment.

Savannah laughs unexpectedly, moving Cole aside and placing a plate of warm cookies on the island. "If you're bored," she glances back at Cole, "I have an idea."

***

Savannah

I dive into a snow bank as three bullets whiz by my feet. Mark pulls me closer to the fallen tree trunk.

"Oh, great, you've got Logan's attention. I thought we lost him back at the driveway."

I check my paintballs and see I have ten left. Plenty.

"No worries, Mark. I have a plan." He looks at me, waiting for me to explain. "Let's just say it involves June and one of our flags." His eyes light up, and his mouth spreads wide.

"You wanna join Blackstone? We could use a member like you."

"Let me be the one who gets Cole and I'll consider it," I joke, rolling on my back, looking up at the window and giving a thumbs up. Mark signals for Davie and Dell to move to the next spot, which is a huge mistake because Cole and Keith change positions and nail them the moment they start running.

"Two down, two to go!" Cole yells out to us. I see June and Mike round the corner looking just like Mark and me. *Perfect*. They make a move toward the wood pile, but Cole is quick and pops both of them in the legs and arms. He turns to Keith, fist bumping, and that's when we move. It's an epic moment. I hope I can replay the cameras and make a copy for myself. Mark swings off to the side and pops Keith in the back of his helmet. I stay low, and just as Cole goes to pop Mark, I nail him in the back three times.

Boom!

Everyone freezes as Cole looks from June to me, wondering what is going on. Then it clicks. He points his finger at me and chucks his helmet to the ground. His smile is dangerous, but all play. I remove my helmet, laughing and feeling very pleased that my plan worked out. Mark fist bumps me, calling out that we won.

"You, come here!" Cole shouts, storming toward me.

"Run, Savi!" Mark calls out. "Run very fast!" I turn and run, but my laughing isn't helping. My boots sink into the deep snow, but I manage to make it to the training barn. I glance over my shoulder to see he's a few yards away.

Once inside, I take in my surroundings and decide an old striped truck in the back corner is where I'll hide. I climb through where the windshield would be and head to the back seat. I hunker down and wait.

I wait and wait and wait…I'm starting to think maybe he had to go inside. Maybe he got a call or Dr. Roberts needed him. Crap…I unfold myself and crawl out the side window. Just as I'm at the front of the truck, he drops down from a rafter, grabs my hips, and tosses me on top of the hood.

I scream out, laughing. "You may have played me, but you forgot one important rule." He undoes my pants and yanks my bottoms, pulling my boots off with them. "You must always be willing to wait out your prey." He unzips his pants, exposing his massive erection. "And you, my love, are my prey." His fingers touch my opening, feeling how turned on I am for him. Just his voice alone sends a flood to the gates. I push all thoughts aside and relax. "So deliciously warm and ready," he whispers as he pulls out his fingers and gently feeds himself inside. My back bows over the hood, my head tips back, and my lips form an O as he fills me to maximum capacity. One hand sneaks up my shirt and palms a breast. "I rather like you like this, Savannah. I'm thinking we should try new places more often."

"I thought we christened my new apartment rather well," I pant as he rolls his hips, hitting every angle he can. I close my eyes, relishing how deep he is, and my tongue darts out, moistening my lips.

"Mmm, that's true." His hands grip my hips as he pushes in harder. I yell out, only fueling his fire. "You have no idea what your sounds do to me." I'm delirious, my vision is going as he keeps up the steady pace. "The way your eyes darken the more turned on you get makes me so hard it hurts." I claw at his arms, just as he yanks me off the roof.

He remains inside of me as he briskly moves us past the holding area and into an office where it's much warmer. I remove my jacket as he sits down on a leather chair with me straddling his lap. He helps me strip down so I'm completely naked. Taking one of my nipples in his mouth, he starts to suck. His other hand roams my feverish skin. I start to rock to build myself back up to where I was. He leans back and swivels me around so my back is to him. "Grip the desk, baby." I lean forward, doing what he says as he stays sitting. "So beautiful." His fingertips run along the length of my spine. He bucks his hips, and my grip slips. "Hold on," he orders while he stands and kicks the chair away from him.

His pace quickens again, each thrust hitting the end of me. His fingers dig into my shoulders and one hand fists my hair.

"Cole!" I cry, not sure how long I'll last.

"I don't care how much," pound, pound, "you try and push me away," pound, pound, "you'll always be mine." Pound, pound. "No more dates, Savannah. No more kissing other men." Pound, pound. "You need something, you come to me."

"It wasn't a date!" I yell out, needing him to understand, but my thoughts get lost as I jump from the ledge. Stars shoot off, sound leaves, and I fall back down to heavenly earth. When I come to my senses, I'm on my back on top of the desk while Cole slips my shirt over my head. I lift my boneless body to help.

"Cole." I stop him as he goes to grab my clothes from the truck. "I didn't go on a date with him. I was doing it as a favor for a friend."

He looks confused. "Friend?" I nod. "Who?"

I sit up, but my bones are like jelly. "I can't say, but I promise you I made it clear that nothing was going to happen. I didn't know he was going to kiss me, and when he did, I felt wrong. Not just because you didn't know, but because it wasn't you."

"It hurt seeing it," he mumbles.

"And it hurt that you broke up with me without hearing me out," I counter, raising my chin. "Makes me think that if the going gets rough, you'll leave me without hesitation."

He steps closer and lowers his face to mine. "I'm

sorry for what I said and the way I acted. It just scares me that you're there in that apartment by yourself, working at that bar with all those men wanting a piece of you. I know I panicked, and in turn it pushed you further away. I want a future with you, Savannah, but not until you're ready. I'm going to back off…" he raises a brow, "*to a degree,* and let you come to me when you decide you're ready for us." His stare is overpowering. "But, Savannah, when you tell me you are ready, be prepared for what's to come." I nod because I can't find my voice. He captures my lips and shows me how true his words are.

The walk back to the house is quiet, with just the sound of our boots. I start to grin, remembering that just an hour ago I pulled one over on him.

"What's with the grin?" he asks, peering down at me.

"I was just wondering how long it will take until the green will wash off your back." I beam up at him. "You know...when I tricked you and won the game." He goes to grab me, but I jump out of the way, laughing. "You know, the game you *forbid* me to ever play again." His smile changes into a devilish one. "Oh, yes, Colonel, I went there." I walk backward, keeping a distance between us.

"You're in such trouble," he says with an evil laugh. "You're in for it now."

I walk up the stairs with a little extra swing in my hips, turning to see him staring at me from the ground. "That's the plan."

Frank and Ryder step out as I reach for the handle.

"Good, Logan, his aunt just arrived at Zack's," Frank calls down to him.

Poor little Ryder looks so scared. "I hope to see you again soon, Ryder," I say, bending down to his eye level. "Don't be nervous of Frank. He just looks scary, but he's a close friend of mine, so you're in good hands." I notice Frank gives Cole a small smile. "Have a fun trip with your aunt." He leans in and wraps his tiny arms around my neck. I can't help but give him a kiss on the side of his head when he pulls away with watery eyes. "Bye, Ryder."

Frank takes Ryder's hand and walks him to the truck, with Cole trailing behind. I wipe away a few stray tears, feeling that maternal need to protect the little fella. I know he'll be fine. I just know he'll be scared from all this, and that's something you can never shake.

"I hate when we get kids," Abigail says from behind me. I nod. She puts her hand on mine. "I know, dear, it *sucks*."

"It does." I laugh at her choice of words. "I've known this little boy all of six hours, but it still hurts seeing him leave."

Dinner is great and just what I needed, an Abigail-cooked meal. Keith stuffs his mouth with my cookies while everyone else eats cheesecake. Soon we retire into the living room while John and Paul set up the poker table downstairs. I take my favorite spot in front of the fire, where Scoot finds me, meowing dramatically and making sure I see how put out he has been since I've been gone. I work hard to make it up to him as his eyes roll back and his legs flop open. *He really has no shame.*

***

Cole

Cole watches as Savannah gives Scoot a good rubdown, and smiles at how he basks in her presence. Everyone is in good spirits, and in no time most are downstairs playing poker while Abigail and June head to bed.

"Savi," Cole whispers. He flicks his head toward the stairs. "Come take a walk with me."

"Where?" she asks, rising to her feet.

"Just downstairs."

He sits her down at the piano, a place where she's comfortable, and moves to stand by the window to watch the snow fall. It always seems to be snowing. He lets out a puff of air, reluctant to have this conversation with her. They were having a good day.

"Ryder seemed to like you."

"He's sweet."

"Are you all right?"

"About Ryder leaving?"

"Yeah."

Her eyes soften. "I've known the kid for six hours. It's sad what happened to him, but we didn't form a bond. Were you worried that I was upset because I lost our baby?"

He nods, wanting to be honest. "Yeah, I was."

"Thank you for caring, but I'm fine."

Cole shakes his head with a smile. He needs to

stop underestimating her strength. He heads to the mini bar and fixes himself a drink, making her a martini just the way Mark does. He sits it on top of the piano and slides in next to her, lifting the lid to expose the keys. "Will you play me something?"

She reaches for the drink and takes a long sip. He wonders if she'll do this for him. It doesn't go unnoticed that she rubs her hands over her lap. She's nervous. "What would you like to hear?"

He brushes her hair away from her face and leans over to give her a kiss behind the ear. "Anything you want."

"Can you sit behind me?" She glances up. "I haven't played in front of anyone in a long time."

"As you wish." He takes his drink and sinks into the large leather seat behind her, angling it so he can study her profile. His stomach is in a knot for both of them. He pulls an ankle to rest over his leg and settles in for a glimpse into this part of her heart.

She closes her eyes and whispers, "Mom." He can almost picture her mother sitting there, encouraging her to play. Telling her how much she loves her. Slowly, a faint smile tugs at her cheeks before she extends her hands and presses down.

Her fingers dance along the keys, making it look effortless. He doesn't recognize the song. It's different at first, but then a note triggers his memory, and he soon realizes she's playing *Yesterday* by The Beatles. She's twisting the melody, adding a little bluesy touch. He likes it, likes it a lot, actually. But what stops his heart mid-beat is when she starts to sing the chorus. Her voice is low but strong. His brandy gets stuck in his throat around the knot lodged there. Setting his drink down, he leans forward and rests his forearms on his thighs, drinking in the intoxicating feeling. It's such a raw and powerful moment.

One finger rests against his temple as he closes his eyes, getting lost in the lyrics. A noise off to his side snaps his eyes open. He slowly turns and he sees his mother cupping her mouth. Her cheeks are wet, the same as his. Savannah, right here, right now, is making progress. She's trusting him with a talent she doesn't share with anyone. He smiles at his mother, who blows him a kiss before she disappears up the stairs.

Moving his attention back to her, he watches in awe as her body moves to the music, and he knows she's born to feel it. He never knew she could play like this. It makes him realize how much he still has to learn about her. Which gives him an idea.

Her shoulders rise at the high notes. Her hair slides off to the side, exposing her slender neck, while her eyes close, pouring her heart into every single word. It's easy to see this is her outlet and passion. He makes a note to look into converting one of the offices into a play room for her. So she can escape and play in private.

When the song ends, she doesn't turn to look at him. She just sits staring at the keys. Breathing in deeply, he clears his throat and moves to her side, seeing her teary eyes. "She was with me," she sniffs, "all the time I was in my prison. I could see her and feel her touch sometimes." A tear slips down, but he catches it before it falls. He doesn't have to ask her to go on. He's heard her tapes with Doc Roberts and how she decided to kill herself at the end, when she lost all hope. "Now she's only with me when I play." She ducks her head down so her hair hides her face. "I'm scared I'm going to lose my memories of her."

"Share them with me, so you won't." He lifts her chin, showing her his eyes, letting her see his sincerity. "Thank you for that, Savannah." He slowly leans down and drops a kiss to her lips, letting them linger a few moments before he says, "You have a lovely voice."

"Thank you." She sighs, closes the lid, and takes a sip of her martini.

He tucks her hair behind her ear, wanting nothing more than to make her feel better.

He offers a hand after he stands. "Come to bed with me?"

Her smile touches the corners of her eyes as she stands, threading her fingers through his. He pulls her in and buries his face in her hair.

"I need to hold you."

Her grip tightens as she turns into him. "Please do."

Chapter Five

"Cole," she whispers, her hand running across his stomach. "Cole, wake up."

"Mmm," he mumbles, pulling her closer and keeping his tired eyes shut. It must be two a.m.

The bed moves as she climbs on top of him. Her hair falls all around as she kisses his chest, his shoulders, his neck, and stopping at his ear. "I need you." His eyes open to her hungry gaze. "To dominate me." A flash of excitement spreads over her face as a wicked smile appears. She sits back on her knees, holding her arms above her head and letting a scarf drop from her fingertips. Oh sweet Lord, this better not be a dream!

He grips her hips, sending her to the side so she's flat on her back. He snatches the scarf and binds her wrists together. "You want me to be rough, baby?" She bites her lip as she gives a nod. "You haven't had enough from last night?" Her legs drop open to show how wet she is. Her eyes drag away from his, and lead a hot trail down to his straining erection.

"Make me scream, Cole," she says, her voice husky. "Make me leave here with a reminder of you."

Leave. That word stings a bit.

He hovers over her and rests his weight on one arm, while the other skims the back of his fingers down along her skin until they meet with the moisture dripping out of her. "You're full of me." He grins down at her. "I love that."

She pulls against the restraints, flicking her hips up so he'll touch her there. He loves how she gives up all control. He needs this just as she does. His fingers push inside, scissoring as they go.

"More," she begs. "Cole, I need more."

He leans down and nips her nipple, making it taut, then blows a stream of air over the top, and she gasps. She's hungry, and he loves it, but he also knows it grounds her when she's feeling lost. The idea of teasing her right now is tempting, but no, he'll give her what she wants. He moves to position at her opening and ever so gently nudges forward.

"Cole!" she nearly shouts, lifting her hips off the mattress.

He steadies his balance and thrusts forward, slamming into her with almost all his strength.

"Yes!" she cries in relief, dropping back in the mattress.

He grabs her legs, hooks them over his shoulders, and pulls her to the edge of the bed so he can stand. He nearly folds her in half as he leans over, getting as deep as possible before he starts thrusting at a maddening rate. Her breasts bounce around in his face, making him even harder. Her bound hands fly forward and run through his hair. He shifts his angle and gets what he's been waiting for, her scream. The scream that makes him pick up speed. She's close, so he pulls out and hauls her up and against the wall. Her hair is wild and sexy, and she pants and cries as he reenters her. He drops her down onto him and uses her body weight to slam down.

"Oh god, baby, I'm gonna come so fucking hard," he growls, biting her neck.

That does it. She bucks, screams, and fists him from the inside. She gives in, tossing her head back. He follows, getting himself as deep inside of her as possible.

He presses his forehead to hers as they both pant and try to catch their breath. Her eyes go from wild with need to satisfied, and it's one sexy look.

"Shower?" he asks, peeling her away from the wall. She shakes her head and he laughs.

He frees her wrists and wraps his sweaty body into hers and kisses her shoulder.

***

Savannah

I head into the kitchen on a search for that heavenly smell I missed so much—Abigail's cinnamon rolls.

"Well, fuck me sideways," Mark says through a bite of toast. "Look who spent the night."

"Morning, Mark," I mumble as I pour myself a large cup of coffee and help myself to a warm roll.

He grins and brushes the crumbs off his fingers. "That it is!"

"Why are you so damn chipper?"

"Because, my sweet Savannah, Cole is winning you back, therefore we all do."

I can't hide my smile as I sip my coffee. Cole strolls into the kitchen, pulling on a t-shirt. I sneak a quick peek at his stomach and remember it flexing when he held me up against the wall, plowing into me like his life depended on it.

"Morning." He flashes me a dirty smile, then grabs my face and kisses me.

"Awww," Mark cues from behind us. "Hey, Keith, you owe me twenty!"

"What?" Keith mutters, coming into the kitchen. "Oh, come on!" He curses. "Really, guys, you couldn't have held out to Valentine's Day?"

"Pay up, dude." Mark holds out his hand as Keith shoves a twenty at him.

"You made a bet on us?" I laugh, realizing how much I miss this place.

Mark jumps up on the counter and bites an apple. The guy never stops eating; it's amazing. "Yup, as to when you'd all get back together." He snaps the twenty in the air.

"I'm getting that money back," Keith informs him as he heads out of the room.

"Whatever, dude!" Mark calls out, then looks back over at us. "Well, I'm out. See ya later, Savi."

***

"You look happy," Jake says as he pours a beer

from the tap. Our shift is going by fast. We barely have a moment to think, it's been so busy. It's eleven, and only now is it dying down enough that we can talk in a normal voice. "Does this have anything to do with a sexy Army man?"

"Perhaps." I bump his hip with mine to move him over. "And Graham?"

"Oh, it's all good." He winks. "He's one dirty bird."

I laugh, but stop when I see his face light up when he looks at someone over my shoulder. I turn to find Cole making his way through the crowd.

It's been four days since I left the house. He whispers something in a girl's ear. She looks at me, then nods as she gets up and frees him an open seat. He removes his jacket and places it over the back, then undoes a few buttons on his dress shirt. Poor guy hates dress shirts. I feel his discomfort. He really is an army pants and t-shirt kinda guy.

I finish with my customer and head over. "Welcome to Zack's," I joke. "What can I get you this evening?"

He smirks. "Brandy, neat."

I nod, then look over at the guy next to him. "And you?"

"Mmm…" he glances at the menu, "Fat Tire."

I place Cole's drink in front of him while Jake grabs the beer for me. "You from around here?" I play with Cole, who grants me one of his sexy smiles.

"You could say that." He takes a sip of his drink. "You have plans later on tonight?"

The guy next to him snickers. "Good luck, dude.

No one has gotten into her pants. Believe me, my buddy has tried many times."

Cole actually laughs, which totally throws me for a loop. Jake looks at me, confused. I just shake my head. "Well, that's good to know." Cole takes another sip of his brandy. "I wouldn't want to have to kill someone."

I chuck my rag at Cole, knowing he isn't joking. He catches it and holds it out at each end. "This reminds me of last weekend."

I grin and shake my head. He's so playful right now, and it's fun. "Where were you?" I ask, tugging at my shirt and nodding at him.

"Meeting," he answers, finishing off his drink. I reach down to make another, and when I look up, the bottle nearly slips out of my hand.

"You!" *she* screams, pointing a finger at me. "I'm going to kill you!"

"What?" I gasp, trying to play catch-up with the crazy charging my way. "What are you talking about?"

She picks up a salt shaker and chucks it at me. I manage to move, and it flies past me. Cole is on his feet, holding a hand up to her.

"Don't act innocent, you bitch." She glances at Cole. "Your whore gave out my apartment number to Don, and he showed up on my doorstep, handing me a stack of cash and wanting me to screw him."

I move to Cole's side. "Christina, I never gave your address to Don! I don't even know where you live."

Jake bursts out laughing. "Maybe he knew your address because you screw every customer we get,

Chris."

"Fuck you, Jake."

"No, thanks," he chuckles.

She suddenly charges me, but Cole blocks her path. Grabbing her arms, he waits until she cries out because of his grip. "You ever touch Savannah, and I'll make sure it's someone looking to do more than have a shitty fuck with you at your door, Christina. Leave my family alone. This is your only warning."

Christina is still heaving with anger when he lets her go, tossing her forward. She spits at my feet, and then Zack appears out of nowhere and kicks her out the door.

Cole ducks down so he's eye level with me. "Are you all right?"

"Yeah." I look around at a few stragglers, embarrassed, though I shouldn't be. She was the one who looked like a fool. "Can you drive me back to my place?"

"Of course." He takes my bag from Jake and offers him a ride, but he has plans with Graham.

Cole parks the car and walks me to my apartment, but stops in the doorway. "I can't stay, baby. I have an early meeting." I feel my disappointment hit hard but push it aside. It was my choice to live here in town. "Hey," he brushes my hair out of my face, "you okay?"

"Yeah, I'm fine."

He leans in, stopping right before he hits my lips. "I love you."

"I love you too, Cole." He gives me a long kiss before turning away.

***

My eyes glaze over as I dip my fry in the ranch dressing, twirling it around then popping it in my mouth. Jake has been talking a mile a minute about Graham and what they've been up to. I love Jake, but he doesn't have a filter when it comes to his sex life.

"Hey, you don't like your burger?" He points his fork at my untouched bacon cheeseburger. I shrug, feeling off. I think I'm just tired. Cole had to fly to Washington to deal with some things in person for four days, so sleeping has been a little hard again. "You're not going to freak out on me again, are you?"

I chuck the rest of my fry at him. "You're an ass." I hand my plate to a waiter who is going by and slip behind the bar, fastening my apron around my waist. "I think I'm just tired—"

A guy comes busting through the door, cupping his mouth. "Honey, I'm here!" I look at Jake, who is very obviously checking him out. *Shameless.* Graham appears from out back.

"No way!" He slams his tray down on the bar and heads over.

"I told you I'd come visit. Now spin," the guy orders, making Graham do a sexy little turn. "Damn, your ass looks fucking fab in those jeans." I see Jake stand, but he doesn't go over. The guy notices, tilting his head at Jake. "Well, looky here, is this…?"

Graham blushes and rolls his eyes. "Be good," he warns.

The guy makes a hungry face at Jake. “That’s like telling the spider to let the fly go, my dear.”

A very pretty blonde walks in behind him, chatting quietly on the phone. “Don’t worry, I’m fine. Okay, I’ll call you later. Yes, I promise. I love you.”

Graham grabs the guy’s arm and walks him over to us. “Jake, this is my cousin, Pete Jones. He’s from L.A.”

Jake's face lights up, and he holds out his hand for a shake. “Nice to meet you. This is my friend, Savi.”

“Well, smack my ass, Graham, you have some hotties here.” The girl tucks her phone away, smiling and joining Pete’s side. “This little love is my best friend, Emily.” He waves his hand around dramatically. “You wouldn’t believe the hell I went through to convince her boy toy to let her come up here.”

“Pete.” She shakes her head, extending her hand to me. “It’s nice to meet you all.”

“Can I get you a drink?” I ask, seeing Jake visibly relax now that he knows Graham doesn’t have a secret boyfriend.

“Dirty martini with three olives for me, please.” Emily checks her phone again as she takes a seat at the bar. “My theatrical friend will have a vodka cranberry.”

I laugh as I make their drinks. Pete is something else; even his hand movements are loud. Emily smiles at her phone. I know that look. That’s the look of some dirty texting, right there. “What are you guys doing up here? Vacation? Skiing?”

She takes a long sip of her drink. "Yeah, something like that." She laughs more to herself than me. "I had a hard last few months, and I just needed to get away. When I heard Pete was coming up here to see Graham, I thought it sounded perfect. The mountains can be so quiet, and I really needed to get out of the city."

I nod, knowing exactly what she means. "I get that."

Her phone buzzes. "Sorry." She turns the ringer off. "My boyfriend's a bit over protective."

I hear Jake laugh behind me. "I think you and Savi have a lot in common, Emily."

"Are you from here? I hear a bit of an accent," Emily asks, fiddling with toothpick.

I shake my head. "Born and raised in New York. Living here for just under a year."

"That's a big move. Do you miss it?"

Do I?

"Honestly, I don't. I think I was meant for the mountains. It just took something big to get me here."

"A man?" She grins.

I lean my hip into the counter. "Yeah, something like that."

"An Army guy," Jake chimes in.

"Oh," Emily eyes go dark, "gotta love a man in a uniform."

I clink my water glass to hers. "Yes, you do."

Pete and Emily stick around most of the night, while I start to feel worse as the night drags on. I barely make it to the locker room when I throw up in a garbage can.

"Oh, sweetheart, are you all right?" Zack asks, rushing to my side. He pulls out a napkin then calls out to one of the staff to bring me some water. "Do you have the flu? It's been going around."

"Not sure," I croak, feeling like I could puke again.

Zack helps me to sit down on the bench. "I'm going to get my keys. I'll drive you home."

"No." I shake my head. "I'm all right, really."

Zack opens my locker and gathers my things "If you're sick, sweetie, I don't want you here."

The idea of going back to my lonely apartment makes me feel even worse. "Do you think you could take me to Sue's?"

He bundles me up and loads me in the car, and we head off to Sue's.

Zack holds on to me as we shuffle up the icy walkway. I'm so damn tired I just want to be in a comfortable atmosphere so I can sleep. Sue meets us at the door, looking worried.

"Come here, honey," Sue whispers, taking me inside and thanking Zack for bringing me here. "Are you hungry?" I shake my head. "You're awfully pale. How about some tea?"

"Okay," I whisper as she sits me down on the couch in front of the fire and removes my shoes. Wrapping a blanket around my shoulders, she helps me lean back so I can lie lengthwise on the couch.

I stare into the fire thinking about how I went from feeling crummy to shitty in a matter of a few hours. It brings me back to York and the poison. My stomach rolls at the thought.

"Here." Sue hands me a cup of chamomile tea

and takes a seat across from me. “Thank you for coming here.” She bats a pesky tear away. “It means a lot.”

“You remind me of her,” I murmur, still staring at the fire. “My mother, she was like a cozy blanket. The moment she was around, you felt wrapped in her comfort and warmth.” I turn to see her glossy eyes reflecting the fire. “As much as I hate my past, it brought me to all of you. I’m incredibly lucky for that.” She smiles at me, but her quivering chin gives away the emotion she’s keeping at bay. “Umm, Sue?”

“Yes?”

I hold my mouth and bolt to the closest bathroom.

***

Cole

Cole walks through the bar, scanning every table for her. Maybe she’s on break. He takes a seat next to a guy who’s telling Jake a story about how he and his friend next to him did karaoke at Chaps last night. The girl seems to be a feisty little thing and keeps her friend in check as he tells the story like it’s a performance.

He waits until the guy takes a breath before he waves Jake over.

“Oh, hey, Cole.” Jake comes over with a glass, holding it up seeing if he wants one. “Savi call ya?”

“No,” he looks around, “why?”

“Look, love, he’s like sex on a stick,” the guy

next to Cole whispers loudly. “Screw L.A., I’m stayin’ right the hell here.” He leans over to Jake. “Is this where all the hotties live?”

“You have no shame!” The girl swats his arm. “I’m sorry, don’t mind him. He’s a fifteen year old perv stuck in a twenty-three year old’s body.”

Jake shakes his head, ignoring the guy’s comment. “She went home sick, think she’s got the flu. Zack took her to your parents’. Guess she didn’t want to be home.”

“It’s not her home,” he mutters, pulling out his phone and calling his mother.

“Hey, honey,” his mother whispers. “I was going to call you once she fell asleep.”

Cole waves to Jake as he leaves the bar. “I’m at Zack’s. I’ll come over. It’s just the flu, right?” His thoughts shoot back to York.

“I think so. She’s just tired and has an upset stomach. She’s gotten sick a few times. You might get sick, honey, you sure—”

“I’m in my car.”

“All right,” he can hear her smile, “drive safely.”

His mother is in the kitchen stirring a pot of chicken soup when he arrives. He gives her a kiss on the cheek and attempts to steal a roll from the baking sheet.

“She’s on the couch.” She nods as he looks over.

He gazes down at her tiny body tucked under a huge blanket, her hair framing her pale face with her hands folded beneath her head. She’s the most beautiful woman he’s ever seen, and she’s his…well, almost his. He leans over to kiss her forehead.

"Cole?" she whispers, not opening her eyes.

"Yes, baby, I'm here. Get some rest." Within seconds she passes out cold again.

"You hungry?" Sue asks from the doorway.

"Yeah." He follows her into the kitchen and takes a seat at the oak table. She sets a hot bowl of soup in front of him with a basket of homemade rolls. She sits across the table from him, trying hard not to show her grin. She's terrible at hiding her excitement. "Out with it, Mom," he says, buttering his roll.

"She came here when she needed someone." Her finger bobs the tea bag in and out of the mug.

"Yeah," he replies, "she did."

"She said I remind her of her mother," Sue beams, but he can see how much that means. His mother always wanted a daughter. His parents tried, but she couldn't get pregnant again. So for Savannah to take to Sue this way means the world. "So…" She clears her throat.

Cole shakes his head, fighting the grin that tugs at his lips. "So what?"

"Oh, Cole!" She bats his arm. "When are you going to ask her to marry you?"

Wiping his mouth, he leans back in his seat. "If it were up to me, she'd have been my wife a long time ago." His mother's hand flies to her chest, swooning in the moment. "But I won't push her into something she isn't ready for. She's well aware I'm going to marry her. I told her to let me know when she's ready, and I'll ask."

"Oh, honey." She laughs a little, hitting her forehead. "Where's the romance in that?"

"Mom, I'm not going to ask and have her say no." He stands to grab the pepper off the island.

"She won't say no."

"She might." He sighs. "Not really sure I can take that rejection."

His mother comes over and places both hands on his shoulders. "That girl came to our house because she is sick, and she was looking for family. She knew you weren't here, Cole, and she still came. The way she looks at you, it's obvious she loves you more than anything else in the world." She pauses to catch her breath. "I watched that woman completely crumble when she thought you were gone. You're her world, so be hers. Don't wait for her to come to you. She's ready, she's just scared. So," she steps back, grinning, "plan something romantic and ask her."

Maybe.

"Yeah, Mom, I hear you,"

"Good." She leans in and gives him a kiss on the cheek. "I love you, honey bear."

"Excuse me," Savannah says faintly, and they both turn to see her slumped into the doorframe, looking exhausted. Cole goes over and feels her head. She doesn't have a fever. "May I get some water, Sue?" She looks over at him. "I'm okay." She tries to smile at him, but he can see she feels awful. "Zack said the flu is going around."

"Here, honey." Sue hands her a glass of water. "You want to try to eat something?"

Her hand goes to her stomach. "No, I just want to go back to sleep."

Cole slips his arm around her waist. "You want

me to take you back to your apartment?"

"No," she shakes her head, making him smile inside, "I don't think I can stomach the car ride." She turns to his mother. "Do you mind if I stay here?"

"I thought that was the plan." She beams.

"Come on, let's go to bed." She sags into him as they walk up the stairs and into his old bedroom. She shuts her eyes the moment she hits the pillow. He removes her jeans and curls himself around her. Breathing in her addicting scent, he falls asleep with the idea of her being his forever.

***

Savannah

I try to be quiet as I bring up the little bit of water I drank earlier. I flush the toilet, wash my face, and brush my teeth, feeling mildly better as long as my stomach is completely empty. I find Cole and Daniel in the kitchen sipping coffee. Sue is making pancakes, which smell pretty good, surprisingly.

"Hey." Cole hops up and pulls out a chair for me. I sit and feel him give me a kiss on the head. I love how affectionate he is with me. I lean into him, seeking his warmth. He feels just right. "How's the stomach?"

"Not entirely sure yet," I mumble, trying to feel it out. Christ, Sue's pancakes smell good.

Cole sees me eyeing them and stacks two on a plate for me. "Eat, it will make you feel better."

Once they hit my tongue I can't stop. I don't even wait for the syrup. The fluffy white cake slides down my throat, hitting my stomach and landing with a hollow boom. Oh my god, I am so hungry! I don't think, just chew. Cole wastes no time refilling my plate, chuckling. I nod a thanks and polish off two more before I feel satisfied.

"I'm going on a hunch here and say your stomach is better?" Daniel teases, putting aside the sports section of the newspaper. I take a few sips of orange juice and feel my energy returning.

"I guess—" I stop when something catches my attention. Part of the entertainment section of the newspaper is flipped over, and one of my most favorite actors, Tim Roth, is up for a new role. Roth. Roth. There's that nagging feeling again.

Cole places his hand on my thigh. "What?"

My head is turning, determined not to lose my trail. "Do you know anyone name Roth?"

He looks a little puzzled. "The only Roth I know is from training up at Camp Green."

I move two steps ahead in my memory, on the right path. "Umm, did I meet him?"

Daniel leans toward us, a little interested in where I'm going with this. "Yes, at the campfire outside. He was one of the recruits I had my eye on, remember, number fifty-nine," Cole says, glancing at his father.

The pieces of the puzzle are all starting to fall into place. "A recruit for the house, right? He would have come to the house and worked?"

"Yes," both he and Daniel answer at the same time, seeing I'm on to something.

There it is, the light turns on in my brain. I'm on top of the fucking memory, and the puzzle is complete! "Holy shit!" Cole squeezes my thigh, coaxing me to go on. "You remember I told you I saw those pictures of you and that blonde woman?" He flinches, but I reach out and cup his cheek. "I'm not digging up this memory to be cruel." I turn to Daniel. "When I was in The American's house, he showed me some photos to prove Cole isn't who I thought he is. He showed me pictures of him and an informant. My point in all this is that The American said he had one of Cole's men take the picture…well, actually, a lot of them." I feel Cole's shoulder twitch.

"You think it was Roth?" Cole asks, bringing my attention back to him.

"Yes, I heard him say his name when I was semi-conscious. One less than sixty," I mutter in disbelief. "The American tried to get me to guess who it was. He said one less than sixty. He also mentioned that he needed him to do well so he would be able to get the location of the house. " Cole's eyes flick over to his father's.

"I think we need to make some calls, son," Daniel's voice is calm but laced with anger.

"Savi," Cole leans in closer, brushing my hair back off my shoulder, "are you feeling better?" I nod, knowing where he's going with this. "Then I need to go. I'll call you later."

"Okay." He leans in and kisses me, then he and Daniel disappear, leaving Sue and me and a stack of pancakes.

Chapter Six

Cole: You at work?

Savi: I am, it's slow.

Cole: How are you feeling?

Savi: Tired.

There's a long pause.

Savi: I'm fine. Did you deal with Roth?

Nothing.

Savi: Cole?

Cole: Will you go on a date with me?

Huh? Where the hell did that come from?

Savi: Sure?

Cole: I've never taken you out on a date. I want to. Tomorrow, be ready at five.

I can't hide my grin. I'm suddenly feeling very excited about my day off. I hoe into my rare steak, licking my lips as I enjoy every bite. Yummy.

"Whatcha gonna wear?" Jake asks over my shoulder, reading my messages as I eat.

"Jake!" I scowl, but it doesn't work when I laugh after. I can't help it. I feel so happy. He snatches my phone and runs to the other side of the bar and starts madly typing.

"What are you doing?" I run after him, dropping my fork, but he's too quick.

He grins as his fingers tap away. Almost immediately there's a ring signaling a message has come in. Jake makes a huff and hands it back.

I glance down and laugh.

Savi: Panties are optional right? I won't if you don't.

Cole: Hi, Jake.

"He knows I wouldn't wear any," I say over my shoulder, heading for the kitchen to return my plate.

Savi: Will I see you tonight?

One step through the door and it hits me like a brick wall. I turn and heave my yummy steak right into the trash can.

"You're still not better?" Zack asks, popping his

head out from behind a fryer. His normally crisp white chef's apron is all dirty because one of the cooks called in sick. He's busy—I can see it on his face—and he's stressed. Zack's is a very busy restaurant. "Savannah, you've been vomiting for four days now. You sure it's just the flu?"

I wipe my mouth with a spare napkin. I feel a little dizzy but stand and give him a smile. "I had the flu, but I'm over it now. I'm actually feeling a lot better, but I ate sushi from the supermarket and it didn't go over so well." I sure wasn't going to admit it was a steak from Zack's. His face twists, thinking about that damn sushi. I knew he'd gotten sick off it once before too. "Once it's out of my system I'll be fine," I assure him.

"Go home, honey, and don't come back till you're better." I start to argue, but he holds up a hand. "You're only going to run yourself down, make yourself worse. One of the deals I made with Cole was to look out for you, and if he knew you were sick and still working..."

"Okay." I hold my stomach, just wanting to get away from the smell. "I'll go."

I let Jake know I'm leaving. "I didn't know you were still sick." I shrug on my coat and pull on my knitted pink hat Abigail made me and lean into the counter, feeling worn out.

"I think I ate sushi too soon," I lie, not wanting to tell anyone I'm still sick with this on again, off again flu.

Jake makes a gagging sound as he hands me my tips. "Let me know if you want me to bring you home anything."

I step up and give him a hug. “Thanks.”

Heading into the night, the breeze feels good across my sweaty face. The nausea is passing, but I’m left completely drained. My stomach has been on a roller coaster of binge eating. My feet are moving, but my mind is dreaming about my pillow. My pocket vibrates and brings me out of my dreamy daze. I remove my mitten and yank it out.

“Hello?” I say without even looking at the number.

“Hey, baby, I was just going to leave you a message,” Cole’s voice washes over me, warming me momentarily. I stop to look into a toy store that has a red and pink display in the window.

“Hey, where are you tonight?”

I hear him shift in his chair. “I’m just wrapping a few things up. Been a long day.” He pauses. “I’m hard.”

I stop mid-step with a grin that makes all the tired feeling leave in a puff. “Oh, yeah?”

“Yeah.” His voice is deep and dripping with need. “I’m thinking about that little scrap of material you call a work shirt. The way your smooth skin looks against the color. The way your breasts pop out the top, begging for my tongue to run along them. I hate that shirt.”

“No, you don’t.” I laugh a little as I run my finger along the window, tracing around a train that a tiny teddy bear is sitting on.

“Mmm,” he chuckles, “I wish you were here. I hate that whenever my office door opens, I have a moment of hope it might be you, but it isn't.” My hand drops as I lean against the cold brick wall and wish he was here too.

"Sometimes…" I whisper, wanting to tell him I think it was a mistake to leave the house, that as much as I need to find myself, sometimes I wish I was back inside the comfort of its walls. I miss everything right down to the way it smells. A horn honks at a car waiting at a green light.

"Where are you?" His voice has lost its husky undertone.

I rub my head, the weariness creeping back in. "I'm walking home."

"Why? Alone? Why now?"

"It's nothing." I sigh and push off the wall, starting my short walk home. "Zack overreacted. I ate something bad and got sick, so he sent me home—"

"So you are alone?" I hear a door close and pull the phone away from my ear, squinting to concentrate on the sound. "Give me ten. I'll be right there."

I stop at a crosswalk. "By the time you get in the car, Cole, I'll be walking into my apartment. I can see it now."

"You should have called me, Savi." His voice is quiet.

I yawn and my eyes water. "Cole, you need to stop worrying about me. Believe it or not, I did keep myself alive for twenty-six years."

I hear ice, then a slow pour of liquid, no doubt brandy. "Sorry," he mumbles. "I know you're perfectly capable of walking a few blocks. But I'll never stop worrying about you, baby. I've lost you too many times to allow it to happen again. Where are you now?"

I chuckle quietly. "Truthfully?" I glance at the stairs. "I'm waiting for the world's slowest elevator because I'm too damn tried to walk up five flights of stairs."

"You want me to come?"

"Always," I respond without missing a beat, "but no, you enjoy your evening. Truly, I'm just going to shower and head to bed. Zack told me not to come back until I feel up to it, so I'm going to sleep in, and I'll see you tomorrow at five for our date."

"Well, don't hang up with me until I know you're inside, okay?"

"Okay." I shove my key into the hole and unlock all the locks. When the door opens, I almost want to cry, I'm so happy.

"Hey, baby," Cole says, sitting on *my* chair and holding a glass of brandy in *my* damn living room.

"How?" I ask, not really caring. I just want to be wrapped in his warm arms.

"Zack called me and said you weren't well. I was already in town, and I was going to come by, but he said you had already left. I thought I'd surprise you." He stands as I come over and rest my frozen cheek on his chest. His arms wrap me up, and I let out a sigh and a long yawn. "Why don't you go get changed, and I'll make you something to eat?"

"Okay." I nod and peel myself away from him.

My shower lasts three minutes. I dry and slip into Cole's army shirt that I love, and then crawl onto the couch where my makeshift bed is made. Cole sets a cup of soup on the table along with some crackers. He sits beside me and encourages me to eat, but instead I lay my head on his lap, pull the covers over me, and drift off to sleep with his hand combing my hair. It's perfect.

"It had been a busy day." His words pull me out from my fog. "We'd just returned home. We had found someone who'd been missing for six months. He needed to be hospitalized, so he didn't stay at Shadows. I was in the middle of playing catch-up with my emails when John brought the file to me. It took me two days before I had a chance to open it." He twists a piece of my hair around his finger. I'm so tired, I can't open my eyes, so I just listen to his story.

"It was the middle of night, pouring rain, when I decided to move to the couch to be closer to the fire." He stops, chuckling a little. "This was back when Scoot wouldn't leave *my* side. The moment I opened that file, your eyes held me captive." His finger gently glides along my jawbone and trails up toward my temple. He makes my skin tingle, heightening my senses. "I think I stared at it for hours. Wondering what your voice sounded like, what your touch felt like, what your lips tasted like. I was completely consumed with your case after that. I turned down two assignments because I got a break on yours, and I couldn't let go." He stops talking, but his hand keeps moving. I almost drift off but fight it as I am enjoying his sudden openness. He seems a million miles away. "When I saw you lying in that bed, so small, and scared…I think a piece of my heart shifted out of place. I didn't realize how strong my feelings ran for you…" He leans down, brushing his lips over my ear. "I'm scared." His whisper nearly breaks me. "I've fallen for you, Savannah. Please catch me."

I start to move—I want to hold him—when I hear him clear his throat. I decide to leave him alone, let him have this moment as I try to control my own emotions trying to surface.

I love this man.

I wake to bright sun blasting through my window, and it takes me a few moments to realize I'm in bed. But what's odd is the sun is in a different place. I stretch my sniff neck to see the time and nearly gasp. Three thirty-two in the afternoon! What the hell? My hand runs along the opposite side, but it's cold. I wonder when Cole left and how he's feeling. My stomach grumbles, forcing me up and out of bed. I really wish it would decide whether it's feeling better or not.

The bathroom still has his scent. I pull back the shower curtain to find his body wash resting on the shelf next to mine, holding my breath at the sight. It's funny how something so small makes me grin like a fool. Why? Because to put it simply, it's just…normal. I grab my phone off the night stand and snap a picture. I attach it to a text message.

Savi: Thank you for giving me a normal moment. I love you.

The kitchen is spotless. He must have done my dishes from last night, and my temporary bed has been tidied and returned to my bedroom. I grab a banana and notice a note stuck to my coffee maker. I laugh, thinking he would know I'd never miss it here.

Good morning, my Savannah, there's nothing better than waking up next to you. I won't lie, I will be late for work this morning. I watched you sleep for about an hour. Have I ever told you you're beautiful? See you tonight.

Yours ~ C

My grin makes my cheeks ache while I stick the note to my fridge so I won't lose it. My stomach rolls, only this time the thought of eating seems pretty damn good. I open my fridge and grab everything I can.

***

"Why am I nervous?" I ask, chucking a sweater out my closet door. I've been through at least six outfits, and nothing is working.

"I think it's sweet," Jake says, coming in behind me and rifling through my clothes. "Here." He holds up a red dress with long sleeves and a crisscross front. "Wear this with your knee high boots." I study the outfit, thinking it's actually good. "Always trust a closet gay. We know best."

I laugh and snatch the clothes from his hand, turning around as I take my t-shirt off to slip on the dress. "What time is it?"

"Four fifty-five. Is Cole normally on—" The

doorbell rings. "The man has a key but rings the bell. A gentleman after my own heart." He bats his eyes at me.

"I'll have you know Keith gave him a key." I laugh, threading an earring through my lobe.

He points. "You want me to get that?"

"Please." I go back to some last minute prepping. I hear Jake make a joke about the flowers Cole must be holding. I take a deep breath and look in the mirror. "Okay."

Cole is standing by the door, while Jake is prattling on about the weather. Cole is dressed in pants and a dress shirt. I know how much he hates to wear them, but damn, he looks sexy in business attire. His gaze finds mine, drops over my cleavage, and tumbles to the floor. A lazy smile appears and my heart skips a few beats.

"Hey, baby." He slips his fingers across his chin, circling under it, with the other hand stuck in his pocket. He slowly moves toward me like a panther hunting its prey, eyes dark and intense. His arms hook around my waist as he drops his lips to mine softly.

"Have her home by eleven. Lucky broad," Jake mutters then shuts the door behind him.

Cole holds my hand to his lips. "I need to tell you something." I look up at him and wait. "I got confirmation that Rodrigo is dead."

"Oh, that's—that's, wow."

I'm...I don't know what I am.

Cole nods. "One down, one to go."

"Three," I correct him, thinking my father needs to be taken out. I grab my jacket and purse.

Cole wraps his arm around my waist, walking me to the door. "Okay, no more talk about that shit. Tonight is about you and me." I lean up and kiss him on the jaw, one of my favorite places.

"Okay."

***

"I can't believe it!" Zack claps his hands together as we walk into the restaurant. "Finally, you two are on a real date! Please come, I've saved the best table." Cole helps me remove my jacket, running his hand down my back and swiping over the curve of my backside.

"This is going to be hard," he growls in my ear. I smile and turn around, conveniently grinding my bottom into his stone-hard erection. I look over my shoulder.

"It already is, baby." I bite my lip, fighting back the lust that's battling with my rational side. We *are* in public. He sucks in a breath as I take my seat. He lets it out as he slips across from me in the booth.

"Hi, Savi." Adam grins and fills my water glass first. "Red's a stunning color for you. Really makes your dark eyes pop." I blush slightly and glance at Cole's face. He's finding it funny.

Ass.

"Thanks, Adam."

"Are you feeling better? Or am I going to need to buy you your own trash can so you can carry it around with you?" he jokes.

"It was nothing," I say before I glance at Cole, who is studying my face. He can I see I'm lying.

"Bad food too soon after the flu."

"2005 *St. Frances*, one of my favorites." Zack holds up the bottle to show us the label. Cole thanks him as he starts to pour the wine. "Adam, stop flirting. Table seven needs water."

"Bye." Adam grins as he walks away.

Zack laughs and shakes his head. "I feel for ya, Logan. You're going to be fighting men off this one left and right your whole life."

"Then I guess we are even," I cut in, and Cole rolls his eyes.

"Dinner will be ready in twenty. I promise, no fish, Savannah." Zack winks and heads over to check in on another table.

Cole holds up his wine glass to me. "To troubled times that only make us stronger. To unexpected love that only makes us fall harder."

"Well said." I clink his glass and take a sip, swirling it around and over my tongue. "It's delicious." I lick my bottom lip, only to get a growl out of Cole. I look over and see his hungry eyes.

"Please don't do that, baby."

I look down to see what he's talking about. "What?"

"That look and the way you lick your lips nearly has me ripping your clothes off right here."

This right here is one of the main reasons I can't get enough of Cole. He's so *animal*. I love the fact that he'll take me whenever, wherever. Not only that, but he tells me what he's thinking without hesitation. This. Is. Incredibly. Sexy.

I twist the wine glass between my fingers. "How would you have me?" I ask so casually people around us would think we were chatting about the food.

"I'd flick up that dress and find you bare and lay you flat on the table. I'd spread your legs and dive in for a taste first. Then grip your shoulders and slip in verrrry slowly." I can feel my chest rising and falling heavily.

"You like taking me from behind," I remind him, encouraging him to go on.

"I do." He takes a drink of his wine while his eyes swipe the crowded restaurant. "It's my favorite position with you."

"Why?"

His grin has devilish written all over it. "It's the sounds you make. They're different, they're more animalistic. It's sexy grabbing your hair and waist watching myself burying full tilt into your tight little opening. Your back curves, your head dips back, and your ass shakes when you want it harder." He closes his eyes in an effort to get control, his jaw ticks, then he looks me straight in the eye. "It's indescribable how much I need it." I find myself panting right there across the table from him at Zack's. In my workplace, no less!

I clear my throat and try to sort my thoughts as Zack and Adam serve our dinner.

"Filet mignon, with sautéed mushrooms and crumbled blue cheese, a side of roasted baby potatoes and fiddleheads." My mouth is watering by the time he's finished explaining. "Enjoy." He nods before backing away and directing Adam toward another table.

The meat is so tender that my fork glides straight

to the plate. I moan in delight at the first bite. The flavors swarm my taste buds, begging me to pair it with the wine. I don't even notice Cole watching me until I tip my glass back and see his gorgeous smile.

"Aren't you going to try it?"

"I'm glad you like it." He picks up his fork and knife, taking a piece of the steak and placing it in his mouth. Cole might be a big guy, but he eats very politely. His parents have raised him well.

We go back to eating and making small talk about the town and its history. We're acting like a normal couple. I love it.

"How're Abigail and Doc?" I ask after our plates have been cleared. Poor Cole tugs at the collar of his shirt, and finally he just unbuttons it. "Feel better?" I grin.

"Yes." He laughs and leans back against the seat.

"Why didn't you just wear what you are comfortable in?" I reach over and take his hand in mine. I trace circles over his fingers, noticing how small mine look in comparison.

"I need to make a good first impression," he whispers, leaning over the table and kissing the back of my hand. "I need to show you I can be more than just a country boy." I slide my hand away and his head flips up. I shake my head slowly, seeing something I haven't before. *Huh.* "What?"

"Cole, I'm not interested in going back to New York. That part of me has died. The very thought of returning there makes me scared as hell." He sighs and gives me a quick nod. I reach for his hand, grabbing his attention. "Honestly, Cole, my heart is with you. Ever since I met you, you've had it. You keep comparing yourself to something you think I am. If that's truly how you see us, then you really don't know me at all."

He looks around to see if the staff is within hearing. "How do I know one day you're not going to wake up and want to go back to the city life? That's not me. I can't do it. I need my mountain."

"And how do I know that one day you're not going to wake and fall out of love with me?" I counter.

"You can't stop loving a piece of yourself, Savannah. You are here." He points to his chest, making my heart want to leap over the table and join his. "Come on." He stands and offers me a hand. He helps me with my coat and leads us out of the restaurant.

His fingers thread through mine as we walk along the sidewalk that's now dusted lightly with fresh snow. Though it's not Christmas, the street is still lined with white twinkle lights, making the town sparkle. He stops us at a window. "You remember this place?"

"Yes." I point to a box now showing a cross necklace. "It was right there. I wear it every day." I pat my chest where it rests against my skin. I turn and point down and across the street. "And right there is where I first met Christina, and you told her we were engaged. I'm not going to lie, that was pretty damn fun."

"Yes, it was."

I pull him down so his lips meet mine and feel him tug me closer. He's warm and tastes like wine. I moan when his tongue massages mine. Snow starts to fall harder, pricking my face and making me shiver.

He clears his throat and wraps an arm around my waist, encouraging me to walk with him. I tuck myself in close, thinking how happy I am when we are together. Things seem to make sense, and so much of my worry floats away when I'm wrapped in Cole's arms.

"Want to get a coffee?" he asks, nuzzling my head with his cold nose. He nods toward a tiny coffee shop across the street. I spot his SUV and reach in his pocket and pull out his keys.

"I actually think I'd like to get back to my apartment," I say, dangling the keys. His eyes darken as he snatches them from my fingers. I laugh as he hurries me over and into the shelter of his truck.

The short drive to my place has me nearly crawling out of my skin. I feel like if his hands aren't on me in the matter of seconds, I'm going to lose it. He pulls into the parking lot toward the back, but when he goes to open the door, I stop him.

"What?" He scans the lot, wondering what he's missing.

The snow quickly covers the windows, hiding us from peeping eyes. I peel off my coat and crawl on to his lap. "Wow, Savannah, here?" I hold his face and swoop down to catch his bottom lip, giving it a nibble. His hands glide to my thighs, pushing my dress up. He growls when he feels I'm once again commando. "Jesus, baby," he mutters as he swipes his fingers between my folds, discovering how completely soaked I am.

I feel almost feverish with lust. I don't know what's wrong with me, but I can't help my hands that are nearly clawing at his belt. He must sense my need, because he lifts up and pushes down his pants and stands up his erection for me. I slide down, tossing my head back with a throaty moan.

He shifts his seat back to give us some more room. I grab the seat, raising myself a little off him, and start moving my hips in a slow, sexy roll. He grabs my ass, feeling the movement.

"Holy Christ, baby," he pants, kissing my neck. "That feels so damn good." I feel my wild side begging to come out. I try to keep it back, but it's taking hold of me. My need for hard, animal sex is surfacing. I squeeze him hard as I flick forward. He grasps my hips and hauls me down. Then I see it. Dominating Cole is starting to show…*perfect!* I squeeze one more time and muster all my will and slow my pace. It's not easy when my head is screaming for me to go on. "Oh hell no," he grunts, shifting me so I'm under him. He flattens the seat as he pulls out. "Up on your knees," he commands. I do, though the space is small and he is so big. I manage and feel his hands grip my hips. He thrusts back in and props one foot up and kneels on the other. He slams me backward…over…and over…and over. I'm so lost in my build-up I couldn't care less if anyone sees the car moving. I *need* this!

"Harder!" I scream. He reaches around and circles the perfect spot, and I go off, screaming his name into the chilly night fogging the glass all around us.

"Fuck, baby," Cole grunts from behind me, "you make me wild. Sometimes I'm scared I'm going to hurt you."

I swallow and try to moisten my dry mouth. "You won't." I shift and pull my dress back down. I scramble to the back seat so he has some room to get his pants on.

We skip the stairs and use the elevator instead. I sink into his side, feeling very relaxed and satisfied.

It isn't until we are in bed, naked and wrapped into each other's arms, that I ask a question. "Cole?"

"Mmm?" he says sleepily.

"Was The American telling the truth about Roth? Was he the one taking the photos?"

Cole pulls me a little closer. "Yeah, he was being paid pretty good to do it too."

"I'm sorry."

He yawns. "When I went to tell him he made it, my gut told me something was off. I'm glad I followed it, I'm even happier you remembered so he could be confronted."

I turn to see him over my shoulder. "So he confessed?"

"Not at first, but when we told him The American outed him, he cooperated. He'll go to jail for a few years, but most of all, the Army is kicking him out."

"Good."

He doesn't deserve to fight.

Chapter Seven

I wake to beads of sweat across my forehead and a strong urge to vomit last night's dinner. I roll out of bed and rush to the restroom. I barely make it before I'm cupping my mouth. I heave and retch for what seems like fifteen minutes. By the time I'm done, I am miserable. Somehow I make it back to my empty bed and sleep for another few hours. The nausea doesn't subside even during my restless sleep. By the time I give in and dry heave, I decide I need to make a doctor's appointment today. I call, and am relieved they're able to see me right away.

The waiting room is quiet, only me and another woman who looks like she's as sick as I am. Shit! I hope I don't have some crazy flu. She glances over and smiles a little, then ruffles inside her purse and pulls something out. She leans over and hands it to me. It's a roll of Arrowroot cookies.

"Try one, I promise it'll help." She nods.

I slip one out and nibble on the end. "Thanks." I try and force the cookie, but it takes a lot of willpower. My stomach is dead set against me feeling better.

"Your first?" she asks, tossing down her magazine.

I roll my head to look at her. I'm so friggin' tired I really don't want to chat right now. "First what?"

She points to my stomach. "Baby."

My eyes widen, snapping me awake. "Oh, I'm not—" I stop when it hits me. "Oh. My. God," I whisper, doing some quick math in my head. I can't believe I am so stupid.

"Congratulations." She stands after her name is called. "Maybe I'll be seeing you around."

"Maybe," I answer, completely shocked by this possibility. I try so hard to stop myself from getting excited, but a smile tugs at my lips.

I pee in a cup and wait with a thumping knee for the doctor to return. So many things are running through my head, one being…what now? A few weeks ago I would have been confused, but today, right now, I know what my heart wants. I want a home with Cole up on the mountain, full of our family. Suddenly, a haunting feeling creeps in when I think I still have two very stressful situations I need to get through—Lynn's court case, and what's going to happen with my father.

The door opening snaps me out of the thoughts screaming in my head.

"All righty, Savannah," Dr. Brown says, adjusting her blouse as she sits across from me. "How have you been since the miscarriage?"

I swallow hard and try to be brave. "I'm doing better, thanks."

"I'm happy to hear that." She opens my file

while I cling onto the seat for fear of falling. "Given the details of your missed menstrual cycle and your urine results, I would say…" She turns a little wheel, concentrating as she goes. "Congratulations, Savannah, you are roughly seven and a half weeks pregnant."

A smile bursts across my face, instantly lifting my mood. "Wow, wow, all right."

"I take it this is something that was planned?"

I nod, thinking we never talked about 'trying,' but we've been trying. No condoms and lots of sex means we were trying. "Yes, we have been. I just didn't recognize the symptoms until today. My work had a flu going around, so I just thought…" I stop and place my hand on my belly, confirming it to myself with touch.

"Where are you working?"

"Zack's, at the bar."

"Hum…" She nods and writes in my file. "Are you still living at the house?"

"Umm, no, I'm living in town," I answer, not sure where she's going with this. Or is this protocol?

She takes off her glasses and leans back in her chair. "Well, since you have had a miscarriage due to high stress, I need to know if there is anything I should be aware of that might endanger this pregnancy." She watches as the bliss drains from my face. "Savannah, I need you to be honest with me, if only for the safety of your baby. You got pregnant very quickly after your last one, and there are risks." She removes her glasses and leans her elbows on her desk. "Remember, everything here is strictly confidential."

"There is." I spend the next forty minutes filling her in on my life up until now, and what obstacles I'll be facing.

"Well, considering all that, I really would like to see you twice a month, and if you feel any discomfort of any sort, you come right in or call me." She hands me her card with her personal contact information. "I really need you to avoid as much stress as possible, though I know that will be hard with what's coming. Maybe you should think about not working?"

"Do I have to?"

"No, I'm just saying if it becomes overwhelming, take some time off. It's just not worth it." She hands me a ton of paperwork and research to go over. "So for now, here are some prenatal pills with some folic acid, you remember the drill. Do you have any questions?"

"Any advice how to fight the nausea?"

"Are you actually bringing up food?"

"Yes, a lot," I admit, remembering this morning.

She scribbles on a pad of paper. "Try eating a piece of chicken or turkey when you wake up. The protein will help take it away. But if it doesn't, take one of these three times a day, and it will do the trick. It will not harm the baby."

I go to leave, but she stops me. "Savannah, I want you to come back in soon so I can get a look at that little peanut. I want to check the heartbeat, make sure this pregnancy is strong from the very beginning."

"I will, but not without Cole."

She nods her understanding.

The walk down the long office hallway leaves me holding onto the wall for support. I've wanted a baby for so long, and here I am pregnant again. I fumble with my purse to pull out my cell phone. I stare at it once I'm outside. I'm not sure what to do first. I start to call Cole, but stop myself as a dark cloud moves in on my celebration. What if something happens again? Do I want to put him through this? Do I wait and tell him after the three month mark? Or do tell him now? My mind is spinning. I block everything else out and let my mind wander as I walk to work.

I'm still lost in my own little world when Jake decides to tell me about his date with Graham. His mouth is moving, but I'm not listening. In fact, I somehow lip read most of my orders. When I don't respond, I get a tap to the arm. Jake is staring at me like I was supposed to have a reaction to his story.

"That's great, Jake." I smile and toss out an empty bottle, replacing it with a new one.

He leans his hip into the bar and crosses his arms. "Is it, now? I wouldn't think Graham almost getting into a car accident is great."

"Wait, what?" I shake my head, trying to recall his words.

"No, I'm lying, but see, you're not listening!" He grabs my shoulders and gives me a little jolt. "What is going on? You're like Night of the Living Dead."

"Sorry." I say with a weak laugh. "I just have a lot going on." I wave my hand at my head.

He makes a face. "Anything I can do to help?"

I serve my client and take the credit card,

swiping it down the machine. "I wish, but no. I just have to make a decision that I'm not sure how to make."

Jake gives me a hug, rubbing my back. "If you need me, you know where I am."

"Thanks, you really have no idea how much I needed to hear that."

***

Three days go by, and I'm still stuck in my routine, not sure what to do. Cole has been busy, so we've only been texting. He hasn't noticed my mood change since I saw him last. I go through ups and downs of being extremely happy, to scared to death, to just plan denial that my body would allow me to get pregnant again so fast.

I work my shift in another blur. Poor Jake must think I'm on something. My customers don't seem to mind so much that I'm not as chatty, which is good because I barely remember my left from my right.

I zip my jacket up and step into the chilly air, and before I know what I'm doing, I'm calling a cab. A short while later, I dial again.

"Keith?" I say once he answers. I can tell he's playing poker because his voice is muffled from his cigar.

"What's up with you? Everything all right?" I hear Dell hooting in the background about his poker hand.

"Can you do me a favor?"

"Of course."

"Tell the *Rambo wanna-be* at the gate to let me pass."

"Wait, you're here? Hang on." A moment later the guy's radio cracks and he waves me into his little heated booth. "What the hell, Savannah? I'll come get you. Stay right there!"

"Yes, sir," I joke, but he doesn't find it funny and hangs up on me.

Headlights blind the booth as he appears moments later. He hops out to open the passenger door, and I rush in, seeking the warmth. He turns the car around and glares at me. We pass through the other two gates before he even speaks to me.

"Do I even wanna know how you got here?"

I close my eyes, whispering the answer.

"A cab? A flipping cab!" he yells at me for breaching the house rules, but I stop him.

"I got him to drop me off a mile and a half away. He wasn't happy about it, but whatever. I hiked in the rest of the way."

He stops the car in front of the house. His hands grip the steering wheel, and the leather stretches under the force. "You hiked in the middle of the night, in the back mountains, where god knows what is out there just to come and visit? Why the hell didn't you call me or Mark?"

I grab my bag and walk toward the door with him close behind me. I know it was the world's stupidest move. I'm reckless for no reason, and I don't know why. Maybe it's because I've been before. "Yes, it sounds stupid, but honestly, the walk felt nice. I needed to clear my head."

"Stupid is not the word I'd use, Savannah," he

grits out.

I turn, feeling tired. "Where's Cole?"

He studies my face while moving past me to open the door. "Should I even ask what's going on?"

"No," I sigh, "not yet." I admit feeling like I owe him that.

"Office was the last place I saw him."

"Thanks, Keith." I drop my bag, remove my coat and boots, and replace them with my flats and hurry that way.

I knock and wait. "Yeah." His voice sounds tired. I open the door and find my Cole hunched over his laptop typing away in a black t-shirt and jeans. Just the way I love him. "What in God's name does anyone want from me at one a.m.?" he mutters without looking up.

"I didn't want to sleep alone tonight," I say softly, and his head snaps up. His face goes from stressed to relieved.

"Hey" his smile draws me toward him. I crawl on his lap and get him to wrap his arms around me. "How did you get here?"

"You seem stressed, Cole, what's wrong?"

"Work. Sometimes I think I need to pass some of it off, but I don't. I'm my own worst enemy." I rub my fingers over the stubble along his jaw, stealing his body heat. "You smell good." He takes a deep breath, then lets out a long sigh. "You have no idea how much I needed this." I lean up to kiss his neck, letting him know I do. "Answer me, Savannah." I know he won't let it go.

"Cab, then hiked it in the rest of the way." His

body turns to stone. "I feel by now I should at least be on the guest list. Rambo out there, who has seen me at least a dozen times, wouldn't let me pass. Pointed his big old gun at me until I finally called Keith to get me through. Honestly, Cole, I need some kind of special pass."

"You took a cab and hiked it here?" I don't have to look at him to know how pissed he is. The vibrating hand on my back is enough to alert me. "Just tell me why."

I shift off his lap and stand in front of his desk, sorting out what I should say. I go to open my mouth to tell him everything, but I can't. My nerves get the best of me. He's watching every movement I make, calculating it, trying to read me. I drop my head and hold back my pesky tears.

***

Cole

Cole can see something's bothering her, but he decides not to push. He's not sure if Frank has called her yet, and if not, he won't be the one to bring it up. The idea of her walking along the dark mountain road makes him want to punch a hole in the cabby's face. Who the hell leaves a woman on the side of the road in the middle of nowhere? He's not sure why Savannah does what she does. Sometimes he thinks she may not have any regard for her own safety, which scares the hell out of him.

"I just wanted to see you," she nearly sobs, twisting his heart. "I didn't want to bother someone to come and get me. It was my choice to move there. You've been so busy, and I've been feeling a little…" She rubs her stomach. If she's still sick, he's going to call Dr. Rice. If there's something going on, he needs to know now. York's face creeps into his mind and makes him uneasy. "I didn't really know what I was doing until I was at the gate. I know it was stupid, but…" Tears start to flow, but she doesn't try to hide them. She looks so tired and small as she breaks down.

"Hey," he stands in front of her, "it's okay, baby. You're here and safe, that's all that matters." He kisses her head as she sags into him. "Why don't you go have a hot bath, and I'll join you in a few? I just need to send off a few emails and I'll be done." She nods as she steps away, looking paler than normal. "Can I get you anything?"

"No." She tries a smile. "I just wanted to sleep here tonight with you."

He loves her words. She has no idea what that means to him, that she feels safe in his home. "Okay, I'll be up soon."

After thirty minutes of writing endless emails that he could quite possibly do right into the morning, he finally turns off the screen. He can't concentrate knowing she's here. He closes up his office and heads for the stairs. He hears the guys laughing downstairs; the poker game must be going well. He's sure Mark is wiping them clean. Tonight they play for money, so Mark's wallet will be that much thicker tomorrow.

He finds Savannah tucked into a little ball on his side of the bed. Her body is curled around his pillow. Her hair is pulled up with a pin stuck through the bun, and the loose pieces are still damp on the ends. He strips and joins her from the other side, forming his body to curve to hers. Her skin is warm and smells of his soap. He kisses her shoulder and along her neck, then his hand travels down her side and slips between her legs, where he finds her ready. She stirs with a little moan. Hell, even when she's asleep, she wants him. He parts her legs and nudges himself up and glides in with ease.

"Mmm, Cole," she whispers, still half out of it. She tries to turn, but he stops her.

"Sleep, baby, I just need to be in you." He squeezes his eyes shut, trying to control himself. She's so warm. The moment he's inside of her, nothing matters but her and him. He lies back down, positing himself so he can stay inside of her as he drifts off.

Something soft brings him out of a dead sleep. Holy shit, it's hot, wet…it feels amazing. A moan fills the room. His eyes are so heavy he can't open them, so instead he reaches out and grabs a fistful of her hair. Her hum vibrating down her tongue makes him buck his hips, pushing deeper. She sucks long and hard, then swirls around him like a cyclone. Three repetitions of that and he's jetting down the back of her throat. She doesn't pull away, just continues until he's finished.

Still trying to catch his breath, she climbs up next to him and tucks herself into his side.

"What was that?"

"Shh," she whispers, "go back to sleep."

He grins, still euphoric from what she just did.

"You're never leaving this bed, you know that, right?"

"Okay," she yawns, falling back to sleep.

The next time he opens his eyes, the bed is empty and there's no head between his legs. No, in fact, his bathroom door is shut and he can hear her getting sick. The toilet flushes as he scrambles out of bed and across the cold wooden floor. He raises a hand to knock when he hears a bunch of pills hit the tile.

"Shoot," she mutters.

He knocks gently. "You all right, baby?"

There's a pause. "Yeah I'll be right out."

The door opens after a minute. She's pale, and her eyes are bloodshot.

Cole shakes his head and reaches for his cell phone. "I'm going to call Dr. Rice. You need to get looked at."

"I saw my doctor three days ago," she says as he reads a text from his phone. "Cole, umm…"

"Shit!" he curses as his phone vibrates in his hand, seeing Frank is coming to the house this morning. "I gotta get going." He turns to look at her. "Savannah, promise me, call Dr. Rice." His head's spinning. He doesn't want Frank to do this this morning.

Her face drops a little but quickly recovers. "Yeah, all right." She smiles and reaches for her bag.

"I'm sorry." He rubs his face and gives her a quick kiss on the lips. "I just worry about you."

Savannah drops her eyes to his chest. "It's fine, don't worry. I will call. I'm going to go say hi to everyone, then I need to head back into town. I work tonight."

"Don't leave without saying goodbye. I don't care if I'm busy. Interrupt, all right?" She nods but still won't look at him, and he glances at the clock. "I need to get ready."

***

Savannah

I watch him head into the bathroom then quickly dress, as doubt creeps up on me. I can't say anything; it would only bring him more stress.

Abigail is in the kitchen feeding Mark's bottomless pit of a stomach. I slip onto the stool next to him and feel my pill kick in. The last thing I want is Abigail or Sue noticing my behavior is off and guess at the pregnancy.

"Hey, Savs." Mark grins, holding a fork full of waffle. "Hungry?"

"Muh." I reach for his wrist and steal the waffle off his fork. "So good." I grin, and he glares at me.

"You dare come between me and my food?" He laughs, spearing another bunch and drenching it in syrup.

My mouth drops as I look over his shoulder. "Umm." He turns to see what has my attention, and I snag his fork, jamming another mouthful of his waffle in my mouth.

"You just went dick deep with that move, Savi. You just asked for it!" He pushes away from the island and wipes his mouth. "I'm going to give you a five second start be—"

I don't wait for the rest of the sentence. I take off and head toward the living room, but see Cole coming down the stairs. "Cole!" I shriek, running over to him and laughing so hard I can barely breathe. "Help!" I wrap myself in his arms as Mark comes running over.

"Give her up, Logan." Mark holds out his hand then rubs his forehead with a dramatic sigh, but I see the amusement in his eyes. "She stole my food, man."

"You made it so easy." I laugh, holding Cole tighter.

Cole's laugh makes me want to hear it again; it's so playful and fun. "What do you plan to do to her?"

"The snow bank is looking mighty fine." He grins.

"You wouldn't!" I turn to look up at Cole and give him the best bedroom eyes I can muster. "How much time do you have before Frank arrives?"

"Oh, you play dirty." Mark lets out a loud *ha* and holds up his hands. "You owe me a cheesecake for this little stunt."

"Deal." I look up at Cole, who's shaking his head at me. "What? You were going to hand me over."

"Never." He smacks my ass just as the doorbell rings. "I gotta go."

"What does Frank want, anyway?" I ask, heading to the door with him.

He doesn't answer as he opens the door and lets Frank inside.

"He's close," Frank says, then stops when he sees me. "Hello, Savannah."

"He? So, who's close?" This may not be my business, but the look on Cole's face is telling me it is.

Frank glances at Cole for help. "Let me talk to Frank, and once I know all the details, we'll let you know what's going on." He steps forward and kisses me on the head. "Please, baby." I nod, reluctant to step over anyone just because of who I'm dating. I know Cole is walking a thin line with having me in his life the way I am. But something doesn't feel right.

I watch them walk off before I hear is voice from the living room. "Chocolate with a strawberry glaze." Mark grins and tosses an apron at me. "And I'll know if you made it with love or not."

I roll my eyes and head to the kitchen.

Keith emerges just as the cheesecake is put in the fridge. He pinches the bridge of his nose. I'm guessing he's tired from his late night of playing poker.

"Is Frank still here?" I ask, hoping he's gone by now.

"Yes, still in the office."

"Any idea what's going on?"

"No."

"And if you did?"

"Then I would know." He smirks down at me, trying to be intimidating, but it doesn't really work anymore. "You work tonight?"

"I do. May I borrow a car to get back to my apartment?"

He laughs. “I’ll drive you home.”

I pull out my cell phone. “You know I am perfectly capable of driving myself back to town.” I send a quick text, and moments later Cole comes into the kitchen.

“You leaving?” he asks, nodding to Keith.

Keith leans against the counter with a devious grin “She wants to borrow a car to drive herself home.”

Cole puffs out some air. “Sorry, baby, that wasn’t in the agreement.” I start to argue, but see him rub the back of his neck roughly, and decide it’s best not to.

“Fine,” I sigh, stepping up on my toes to give him a kiss goodbye. “Anything you wish to share?”

“Not yet,” he says, resting his chin on my head and holding me close. “I’ll call you later. I’ll stop by if I can.”

“I love you.” I’m teary eyed. *Sweet Jesus, Savi, grow a pair.*

“Hey,” he says, pulling back to stare down at me, “what is going on with you?”

Keith leaves the kitchen, saying he’s going to get the car ready.

Frank walks into the kitchen with a phone to his ear. “Logan, round up Blackstone. Jose's trying to get into Guatemala. Be ready in thirty.”

Jose! Everything around me starts to look funny. I step backward, feeling like I’m falling. Sounds are mixing together. I can’t separate them. I don’t feel Cole pull me to him, I just know he has me around the wrists, trying to get me to look at him. Mark appears, but his voice is funny, and black spots mar my vision. Then suddenly everything comes rushing at me. I start to panic, my breathing erratic. This is my biggest fear. Cole going to fight. That's why I got in the way with his plans to get recaptured last time! I wasn't prepared for Jose to reappear.

"Savannah! Look at me." Cole's voice cuts through my panic. "It's an easy trip, I promise. He's alone, and we're just going to pick him up and drop him off in Washington. It's—"

"No." I grip his sweater like he's trying to get away from me. "Please, Cole, send someone else! Don't leave me!" I'm crying now, and he goes blurry as my tears spill over. His eyes pop open with the fact I went from zero to ten in a matter of seconds. "If it's such an easy trip, send someone else."

"Baby, it's going to be fine." He lowers his voice to calm me, but it doesn't work. I wiggle free, holding onto the counter. "Mark, please!" I turn to him for help. He looks so sad but doesn't say anything.

"Ready!" John yells from the other room.

I want to puke, I want to scream, I want to crawl out of my own skin, I'm so frigging scared right now. A loud sob escapes me, and I grab my mouth in an attempt to contain the rest.

I'm losing it.

Mark holds up a hand to Paul, who is coming in the kitchen.

"Savi, you need to hear me. Everything is going to be fine."

"Like last time! When you left and—" I hold my rolling stomach.

Cole takes a step closer. "I've been doing this a long time. What happened last time was—"

"Our baby needs a father, Cole!" I blurt out. He freezes as his eyes drop to my hand holding my stomach.

"You're…"

"Just over seven weeks," I whisper, seeing his eyes crinkle in the corners, then a huge smile appears. He leaps forward and wraps me in his arms.

"Oh my god!" he whispers into my neck. "I love you, Savannah, I love you so damn much!" *Oh my god, did I just admit that I'm pregnant?*

"Don't leave me, Cole, I won't be able to handle it, not now, not again!" I shake, unable to calm myself. I need to hear him say it.

"I'll talk to Frank, see what I can do." He pulls back, drying my cheeks with his thumbs.

We both turn when we hear Mark shuffling around, doing some kind of dance. Keith comes in, and his brows are squeezed together in confusion. "Fuck me sideways, brother! Hand it over. Fifty big ones! Damn! I have one hell of a horseshoe stuck up my ass."

Keith's mouth drops when he sees Cole's hand on my stomach. "Really?" He beams. "I'm going to be an uncle?" He hugs me with a laugh. Then he turns to Mark. "The missus is pregnant, you know what that means?"

"Bubble wrap and a helmet," Mark jokes, and Cole laughs.

"Means more trouble for all of us. You imagine if they have a girl? Another Savannah?"

Mark's face drops. "Shit, we're all screwed."

I roll my eyes. "Right, so be nice, or I'll sic our little one after you."

Mark comes over and gives me a huge hug. "Congrats, Savi!"

"Thanks, Mark." I sigh and try to get a handle on what I just spilled. "Let's keep this between us right now."

"Do I wanna be Uncle Mark? Or Uncle M?" Mark thinks aloud as he leans against the counter.

Frank returns, and Cole leads him into the living room. I take a seat on the stool as my head spins. What if Frank doesn't agree to let him stay behind?

"Either way," Mark says, setting a glass of water next to me, "we won't be gone for more than fifteen hours."

I sip the water and think this is how it's going to be whenever he leaves. I'm always going to wonder if he'll return to me and our baby.

"Frank's team is going to step in and help out Blackstone," Cole says, addressing Mark and Keith, then he looks at me, "since I'll be staying behind this trip."

I drop my head to the cool counter as the weight of the world rolls off my back momentarily. The men quickly leave, and the house becomes quiet. Cole walks them to the chopper pad, giving instructions. I stay behind. Taking a seat on the large sofa, I curl up under a blanket when I feel my ear being nuzzled by a little pink nose.

"Hey, big guy." I reach up and pull Scoot onto my lap. He snuggles down into the fleece blanket with me and purrs a soothing rhythm. My eyes soon grow heavy, and I drift off.

Chapter Eight

Cole

Cole slips his phone into his pocket and heads into the living room where Savannah is lying on the couch. He lifts her legs and rests them on his lap, then places his hand on her belly. "You awake?" he whispers.

"Mmmhmm." She opens her heavy eyes. Scoot is not liking his nap being interrupted, and he shoots Cole a rather rude look.

"I spoke to your doctor," he says, gently rubbing circles. "You've known for about four days?" She bites her lip and her chest falls heavy. "Okay," he sighs. "She tells me you need to be careful with stress. So what happened earlier is that going to be an issue every time I need to go away?"

She sits up, lowering Scoot to the ground, and pulls her knees up to her chest. He recognizes it as her defensive move, so clearly they have a bump in the road here. "Baby, I have to be able to do my job, but I have to know when I leave you're going to be okay with it too. Maybe you need to talk to the doc about this, maybe—"

"Oh my god, Cole, no more doctors!" She stands and moves over to the fireplace, picking up a model car from the mantel. "I'm so tired of talking to people. Bottom line is you have no idea what it was like for me when you were taken."

"Don't I?" He leans forward and rests his arms on his legs. "If I recall, you pranced off to New York to find answers, only to get yourself taken. Seems to me I'd have an idea of what you went through."

She puts down the car and whirls around to face him. "Really? Did you see me held hostage, kneeling on the floor while a machete sliced through my neck? No. You were at most a day away from me, working on the actual hunt to get me back. I had to stay put and wait while everyone tiptoed around me, not wanting to stress me out." Her voice drops a bit, and he sees a painful flinch flash across her face. "Not that it helped any."

He sighs, knowing she's still hurting from that day; they both are. "So where does that leave us? I can't not travel, Savannah. Blackstone is my life." As soon as the words leave his mouth, he regrets them, and he sees her withdrawing. "I mean, it's all I've had for so long, I've built my life around it. I can't give up a family business just so you won't worry. I could drive to town and be hit by a semi."

She runs her hands through her hair and lets out a long breath. "I have to get to work."

He stands and raises his hands. "Seriously?"

"Cole, it's a little different, me working at a bar

and you doing some crazy G.I. Joe manhunt for a guy who beats women within an inch of their lives and has killed men for looking at him the wrong way."

"I don't like you working when you're pregnant, Savi."

"Well, then, I guess we both don't like each other working, but neither of us is going to stop, right?"

"Savannah…" His voice has an edge to it.

She grabs her bag, then turns to look at him. Her face is so different. "I don't want to fight with you, Cole. This is not how I saw this moment going. I think we both need space to think."

He hurries to block her path. "Think about what, exactly?"

She drops her head and lets her hair make a curtain around her face. She takes a moment to gather herself, then looks up at him with red eyes. "Everything."

"Ready?" Mike asks from the entryway.

"Yeah." She waves. "I'll talk to you later."

"Savi," he barks, grabbing her hand and hauling her back to him, "don't you dare find some reason to pull away from me. You can't tell me you're pregnant and then withdraw. I don't know what's going on with you, but you better start talking soon. I'll see you later on tonight, so be prepared to talk then." He grabs her face and kisses her. She fights it for a moment, then gives in. He gives her belly a little pat before he lets her go.

"Mike, call me the moment you drop her off at home, and wait and drive her to work. I don't want her walking in the snow," he warns as she shakes her head toward the door.

"No problem, Logan, I will." Mike smiles at her and offers to take her bag.

He watches them leave, then pulls out his phone to call Frank when June appears from the kitchen. Her smile tells him she knows about the baby. Good thing about June, she can keep a secret, even from Abigail, if need be. She comes to his side at the window and gives him a pat on the back.

"She's scared, honey," she says quietly, not looking at him. "It was truly horrific what she went through here. That poor woman shut down and wouldn't let anyone in, but it's how she survives. When she saw that video and then lost the baby all in a matter of minutes, oh Lord, it was…" She puts her hand over her mouth and shakes her head. "It was a nightmare. It scarred her. She still isn't right. I can see it in her eyes."

Cole nods, knowing she's right. "I can too. But I can't not work, June. I just can't, it's what I do."

"I know, Cole, and she does too, but I think this job is especially painful because it has to do with her. It'll take some time, but she'll come around. I bet you anything when you see her tonight she'll be better."

He rubs his aching head, wishing he could just pack up her shit and move her back home. "Let's hope."

"Congratulations, by the way." She smiles. "I promise I won't breathe a word."

"Thanks." He lets himself think about the little one growing in her belly. "You think you could help me with something?"

"Anything."

***

Savannah

I am tired and just want to hibernate in my little apartment. All afternoon I've felt like crap over my conversation with Cole. Never once did I plan to tell him I was pregnant and then get into an argument. Of course I'd never ask him to leave the Blackstone team. It's just with Jose, if anything happened to him, it would be my fault again. I feel like crying, but Jake bumps me in the hip, making me move so he can ring in his order.

"Thirty minutes left and the place is still packed," he groans. "I'm so flippin' beat, and all I can think about is passing out in Graham's goose down duvet. I swear I'm only with that man for his blanket. Well…" he gives me a smirk, "that and one other thing."

"I miss my neighbor," I pout, fighting down a surge of emotion. Seriously, this whole jacked up hormones thing is getting a little old.

His hands fly to his hips. "You think I don't lust over your coffee? Or your chocolate chip cookies? Oh!" He smacks my arm. "That reminds me. Keith was in here snackin' on one earlier. What the hell, woman?"

I chuckle, rolling my eyes. "He had some frozen from a while ago. Trust me, I've heard all about it from Mark."

"Mark doesn't count. He could eat an entire cow and have room for seconds. He doesn't love treats like I do, and I have no one making me any…" He gives me sad eyes and sticks out his cute little lip.

"Fine, the can on top of my fridge."

"Hang on," his eyes narrow on me, "you have some cookies in your apartment, like, right now?"

I open a beer and hand it to a woman. "I need them to bribe Keith with." I shrug, feeling no shame. I turn to my next customer and want to sigh, but I hold it together. "Hello, Don. Scotch, neat?"

"You know I come to this place just to see you make my drink." He smiles and places his credit card and his hotel key side by side in front of me. "I love how you wait on me."

I hold back my rolling stomach as I take the credit card, leaving the key behind. When I turn back around to hand him his drink, I jump when I see Cole sitting right next to him.

Don slides the key at me. "You know you want to take it, sweetie." I rub my face as my tolerance for this man drains out of me.

"Are you going to want another? We close in fifteen," I say rather rudely. Of course he doesn't notice. He's too busy staring at my chest.

I turn to Cole, whose jaw is ticking. I know he could punch Don once and kill the man. "Brandy?" I pull out a glass.

"Please." He nods, rubbing his face. He seems as irritated as I am. "How are you?"

I pour him a double, slip a napkin under it, and slide it over. "Tired." I shrug.

"I can fix that, doll," Don cuts in, waving his

room key at me.

Cole goes to speak, but I place my hand on his. "Trust me, Don, you're not going to want anything to do with me in nine months."

He makes a disgusted face. "Fuck off, seriously?"

"Seriously," Cole warns. "Show some respect."

Don takes a moment, not listening to him, then shrugs. "I'm into kinky shit."

Cole turns to look at him, and my blood runs cold. I actually fear for Don's life right now.

"Cole," I reach for his arm, "please." He squeezes his eyes shut, calming himself.

"We're done! Thank fuck!" Jake cheers behind me. "Here." He slips my tips into my pocket, then reads the situation. "Umm, I'll punch you out and get your things."

I take my apron off and wipe down the bar. All the while Cole and Don sit side by side, both watching me. Don has some balls or he has a death wish, or maybe he's just clueless, but he doesn't move away from Cole.

"Great job tonight, Savi," Zack says, coming in through the dining room area. "Hey, Logan, so the rumor is true." I know they're referring to the fact that Cole didn't go with the Blackstone team.

"It's the first time in twelve years." He glances at me. "Had a good reason to stay behind, though."

I give a small smile, letting the good feeling spread through me.

Don flicks his head at me. "Last chance, doll." He flicks his room key at me, hitting me in the chest.

Zack manages to get between Cole and Don in a flash. “Easy, Logan,” he says calmly, then turns to Don.

“I’m going to give you exactly one minute to leave this bar, before the Green Beret behind me bends you small enough to fit inside your scotch glass.” Don looks up at Cole. “I’ve heard you’ve been making trouble for my staff, and I’ve let it go because they’ve been handling it, but what you just did there was crossing the line. Get out, and don't show your face in here again.”

“Are you kidding me? Do you have any idea how much money I spend here?” Don grumbles, grabbing his jacket. I hand him his card and his bill to sign.

“I don’t care, don’t need your money,” Zack says, pointing to the door. “Leave.”

Don looks over at me and grabs his crotch, making a total ass out of himself. “Your loss, doll. Could’ve been epic.”

Cole starts to move, but Zack grabs Don by the jacket, yanking him toward the door.

“Always exciting since you started working here, Savi.” Jake laughs, trying to bring the tension level down a little. “Here.” He sets my things down on the bar top. “Graham is waiting for me. I’ll call you tomorrow.” He gives me a quick hug, says bye to Cole, and heads out front.

“You done?” Cole asks, shrugging on his jacket. I can feel the anger pouring off him. I want to kick Don’s ass for putting him in this mood. I switch my shoes, tug on my jacket, and grab my bag, coming around to meet him on the other side of the bar.

"Come here." He pulls me over, wrapping his arms around me. "I love you." He kisses my head and lets out a long sigh. "More than anything."

"I love you too," I whisper.

Back at my apartment, I snuggle further under my blanket on the couch. Cole is next to me while we watch *Zero Dark Thirty.* I ask a few questions about how real certain parts are. Kind of neat asking someone who really knows the truth. "Are you upset you're not there?" I ask guiltily.

He shifts from behind me. "A little, yes. I get a high from the hunt." His hand slides over my stomach. "But I'd be craving to be right here the whole time, and that would endanger the team." My hand covers his. "I know you're scared, baby, and we have some things that need to be dealt with before we can move forward, but we'll do it together, all right?"

I turn, loving his words. I reach up and run my fingers over his stubble. "All right."

"All right?" he asks, as if he'd been waiting for a fight. I nod with a smile.

"I won't lie, I am scared, but if I know I have you with me, then I'll be all right."

He leans down, capturing my lips and giving me one hell of a kiss. I have to push him away when my phone goes off and won't stop ringing.

"Hello?"

"Hey, honey." I mouth 'it's your mother' to Cole. He nods and looks back at the movie. "Sorry for calling so late. I was wondering if you are you free tomorrow. I was hoping we could all have dinner at the house. What with you working then having the flu, I thought that now since you're feeling better we could all get together."

"Sure, I'd love that. I could trade shifts with someone. I could do the morning instead—"

"Actually…" She pauses, then there's a strange noise.

"You have the night off, Savi," Zack says into the phone. "Go spend time with your family." I laugh and glance up at Cole, who looks at me funny.

"Thanks, Zack, I appreciate it."

"Sure thing."

"Hope that was all right?" Sue asks, feeling me out. "Daniel and I just ran into him."

I smile. "Of course. I'm looking forward to tomorrow."

"Wonderful, me too. Either Mike or I will come pick you up whenever you're ready."

"Okay, thanks. Bye, Sue."

I slide my phone on the table and snuggle back into my warm spot. My apartment can be so cold sometimes. Cole's hand immediately lands on my belly. I sigh, thinking how lovely it feels.

"What did my mother want?"

I tuck the edges of the blanket around me tighter, feeling a draft from somewhere. "She wants to have a family dinner tomorrow night. She even got me out of work tomorrow."

"Mmmm, you back at the house?" He nuzzles my hair, breathing in. "I love my mother even more right now."

I tip my head back and look into his dark eyes. His smile reaches the corners, making them crease along the edges. His stubble is the perfect length, and my fingers twitch as I reach up to steal a quick feel. He leans in, kissing my hand. He shifts so we're lying down, his body flat along the back cushions, with me staring up at him. His hand sneaks up my shirt and runs along my side.

"Hard to believe there's a little something inside this tiny belly of yours." He stares at my stomach, fascinated. "Did you get to see Sim when you had your appointment?"

"I'm sorry, what?" I laugh. "Sim?"

"Yes, she and him, therefore, 'Sim,'" he says, deadpan, circling my belly button with his finger. I hiccup, trying to contain my giggle fit. "Hey, now, stop. You're going to make Sim sick with all that shaking."

"Oh, Cole." I full out laugh and bring up my legs to stop the hurt. "Stop, I can't breathe." I roll onto my side and take slow breaths.

"Finished?" He pokes at me. "Well?"

I roll back over, and he resumes his circles. "No, I haven't. I've just had the urine test so far. I have an appointment in a week."

"First, *we* have an appointment. And how do they know? You may not be."

"Oh, trust me, baby, that stick had two neon strips that could light these mountains right up."

He grins, making me confused. "You called me 'baby.'"

"Is that bad?"

"No, I liked it."

"Baby," I joke, biting my lip playfully.

He swoops down and nips at my lip, freeing it

momentarily before he draws it into his mouth and sucks softly. He pulls back, eyes dark as night, and checks the time on the phone. "What if I called Dr. Brown tomorrow and ask her to do an ultrasound?"

"You can't just call—" The look on his face tells me otherwise. "If you can make it happen, Sim and I are on board."

His face breaks out in his 'she gave in without a fight' smile. I yawn, turning into his chest, and he pulls the covers over us and holds me close.

"What do you think we're having?" I ask, as sleep begins to creep over me. Cole tucks me under his chin.

"Girl," he says in a matter of fact tone. "The world really needs two of you."

My heart swells to the point of pain. I move to give him a kiss on his chest. This man has made me feel more love in just a few months than I've ever felt from another man in my whole life.

***

Cole looks completely at ease in the sea of pregnant women. He worked his magic and got us an early afternoon appointment at the hospital with Dr. Brown. How he did it is beyond me, but I don't care. I just want to see our little baby.

"Here," Cole pulls out a bottle of water from my bag, "you should drink this."

"I'm all right," I say, scanning a magazine on breast feeding verses formula. He takes off the cap and nudges it in my hand.

"You need to drink more water. You should be

on your second one of these by now."

I chuckle and take the water and finish off the bottle. "Someone's been doing their homework," I tease, loving that he has been.

His hand falls on my thigh and gives it a light pat. "I want to know everything so I can take care of you two."

"Ms. Miller," the nurse calls out, glancing around the room. Cole mumbles something as he takes my hand and leads me into the hallway.

"Hi, Savannah, my name is Tracy. I'll be helping you today. First, I need you to give a urine sample, then you can meet me and…" She looks at Cole.

"Cole, the father." Cole rubs my belly from behind.

"We'll meet you in room four, okay?"

After I fill my cup, then get my blood pressure and weight taken, I find the door to the room where Dr. Brown is already waiting and deep in conversation with Cole, who is firing questions.

Of course, I smirk. He's so cute.

"Hello again, Savannah," she says as Cole pulls out a chair for me. "You look a lot better than the last time I saw you."

I shift, remembering how sick I was then. "Yes, the pills are helping a lot."

"All right, so let's get you undressed from the waist down and see how the little one looks."

Cole nearly doubles over when he sees the probe that's about a foot long slide inside of me. He's three shades of white until the little pulsing ring appears on the ultrasound machine. He suddenly grabs my hand and holds it tightly, but his eyes stay stuck to the screen.

"Strong heartbeat," Dr. Brown says, clicking a few buttons, "and I would say you are right around eight weeks, a little further along than I thought. Which will make your due date about early August. Congratulations, you two, you have a healthy looking baby. Let's keep it that way."

"You gave the doc a run for her degree," I joke in the car after our appointment, digging in a bag of trail mix to steal the chocolate chips before he notices. He scoops his free hand in, pouring a handful into his mouth while keeping his eyes on the windy road.

"I had questions," he says with a shrug. "And I don't wanna see you with a cup of coffee."

"Cole, she said a small cup is fine." I roll my eyes. These next seven months are going to be interesting.

"You need to eat more meat too." He gives me a sideways glance. "She said your iron is low, and that's one of the reasons why you're so tired."

"Cole—"

"Speaking of being tired, you should think of cutting back your shifts—"

I snap the lid on the trail mix and toss it down by my feet. "Please don't start, Cole. I love my job."

He sighs. Running a hand through his hair, he reaches for my hand and brings it to his mouth, kissing the back of it. "Sorry, I'm trying really, *really* hard not to let my controlling side take over. But when you toss in our baby, it's even more of a struggle. I just want you to get as much rest as possible, and this pregnancy to go smoothly."

"Look, I'll make you a deal. When I feel work is too much for me, I'll stop."

"No offense, baby, but you're incredibly stubborn." I see him fight a smile, and he uses my hand to hide it.

I want to be truthful, for him to see I'm taking all this seriously. "I learned my lesson the first time, Cole." His smile fades. "I promise when it gets too much, I'll tell you."

"All right, but if I see you're fading, I *will* say something." He rolls his window down to speak with the guard at the gate.

***

The baked apple smell hits my nose when we walk in, and my stomach forgets all about the snack on the way up. I grin when I see June's green scarf hung over top of her black pea coat, and Abigail's boots next to one of Scoot's many beds. Keith's snow pants and mitts are by the door. Everything is as it should be, just as normal should be. I close my eyes, savoring the comfort that is this house. *It's perfect.*

"You coming?" Cole asks. I hold up a finger, asking for one more moment. "You all right?"

I open my eyes, seeing his puzzled expression. "I'm just thinking."

"About?" he asks, taking my hand in his.

"Things." I lean up to kiss his cheek. "Happy things."

"Hi, honey!" Sue beams with delight as we round the corner and see everyone in the living room enjoying some afternoon drinks before dinner. She stops in front of me, studying me for a moment, then leans in and gives me a hug. "Are you feeling better?"

"I am, thanks." I hug Daniel after he comes up behind her.

"See, nothing to it!" Mark hands me a martini with a wink. "Thought you could use this, just until you're ready to tell."

"Does this mean…?" I look at Cole, who grins.

Mark tosses his hand in the air in excitement. "Yes, as of six fifteen this morning, Jose Jorge is on U.S. soil, behind bars, with a shit load of charges against him. He'll be spending his next three lives as someone's prison bitch."

"Well, that's something to celebrate!" I cheer ecstatically.

"We have lots to celebrate," he says over his shoulder, heading for the kitchen.

Cole keeps me close to his side. Every so often his hand slips over my belly, letting me know he's thinking about little Sim.

"Hey, guys." Keith joins us, checking his phone. "I hate to ask this, but can I steal Logan for a moment?"

Cole leans in to give me a quick kiss. "I'll be back." I nod and watch the two hurry off to his office.

I mingle with everyone, sipping my water. Davie and Dell are telling a story from a few nights ago when they were in town at Chaps. I pretend to listen, but I'm more interested in where Mark is hurrying off to. I scan the crowd and see Daniel is gone too.

Where the hell is everyone? Oh no…is something happening? My father?

"Savannah?" Mike calls from the entryway. I whirl around. "Can I steal you for a moment?" A strange feeling creeps over me as I sit my drink down and hurry over to him. "Let's take a walk." He waits as I get ready, growing more nervous with every moment.

He opens the door to let me go first. It's dark and the temperature has dropped, so I wrap my scarf around my neck and wait for him to lead the way.

"How have you been?" He guides me across the driveway toward the woods.

"Cut the crap, Mike. You didn't ask me out here to see how I'm doing."

He smiles and shakes his head. "Yeah, you're right." His face changes, softening a little. He points to a glow in the woods. "Follow the light, Savannah." He nods for me to head in that direction.

Puzzled, I start to walk. After several steps I hear Mike whisper something. I turn and look back, but he's walking away from me. What's going on?

I stop at the tree line and take in all the glass lanterns marking the pathway. Drawn by their light into the woods, I follow them, thinking how strange it is I'm not with anyone. I take comfort in knowing someone will be watching me. The further along I go, and the more I see the lanterns ahead. They are so pretty. Their warm twinkle leads me deeper into the woods, and the soft snow falling from the trees is soothing. Flames flicker with the tiny breeze, making the forest look magical. If I were to write a fairytale, it would be just like this. Heavy snow weighing down the branches, little hues of light with a glow just bright enough to look warm, an untouched forest just waiting to spill its secrets. The only thing missing is…I turn a bend to a clearing and see him…*oh!*

Chapter Nine

Cole stands by an open fire, and the orange glow makes it easy to see his smile when his eyes lock onto mine. Dozens of candles are nestled into the snow banks, creating a magical scene. He holds out his hand as I get closer.

"Hi." I grin, loving how just one look from this man makes my insides melt. "It's so beautiful, Cole. What's going on?"

He looks down at me. "Do you remember what happened here a few months ago?"

"Of course, it's where we said we loved each other," I say, thinking I might have figured out what's happening.

"Savannah, I've been in love with you from the first moment I saw your picture. It just took me a while to realize what that feeling was." His free hand runs down my temple. "Your eyes are so beautiful, it's as if someone removed a star and made you from all its beauty." My breath catches as my eyes water. "There has never been anyone I've ever wanted more in my life until I met you. You've opened my eyes, made me see that my life at the house doesn't mean I can't fall in love and be happy." His hand moves to my belly. "Baby or no baby, you've always been mine." He bends down on one knee, pulling out a light blue box. "Savannah Miller, I swear under a thousand stars that I love you, and will fight to the end to make you happy." He kisses my left hand. "Will you marry me?" He slowly opens the box, revealing a sparkling princess cut diamond.

"Yes! Yes!" I cry, laughing, as my heart pounds a tattoo inside my chest. He slips it on my finger, then jumps up, lifting me off the ground spinning me around.

"I love you," he sighs, pressing me tightly against his chest, his voice muffled by my hair. He pulls back, looking down at me. His eyes are glossy, making mine water even more.

"I love you too, Cole." I take in my surroundings and see all he did to make this moment perfect. "I can't believe you did this."

"I'd do anything for you." He steps up, grabbing my face and kissing me with such passion it takes my breath away.

"Well?" Mark's voice chirps out of Cole's pocket. I laugh at how normal it is that he'd have a radio in his pocket.

"Raven One to Raven Two," Cole winks, "she said yes."

The roar that erupts from the house can be heard all the way up to where we are standing.

"You ready to tell the family about our baby?" He holds my hand as we walk along the snowy path down to the house.

I take a deep, slow breath through my nose, drawing the scent of the forest in deeply, letting this amazing feeling rush through me and around me. "I am. I can't wait."

Everyone hugs, kisses, and cheers when we return to the house. It isn't until dinner is finished and Mark digs into the dessert that Cole stands, taking my hand and helping me out of my seat.

"Can I have everyone's attention, please?" Cole clears his throat, and the noise dies down. "First, I want to say thank you to everyone who made my proposal happen. Second, Savannah and I have something we'd like to share with you." He waits for me to say it, but I can't. I'm next to tears with happiness. So Cole slips his hand over my belly, and everyone's eyes drop.

"Oh my goodness," Sue says, grabbing onto Daniel, who is already tearing up. "Really?"

"Really," I choke out. "Just over eight weeks."

Mark turns to Keith. "You still owe me, dude."

The whole table starts to laugh, and anyone's thoughts about the tension around the last time I was pregnant quickly fades, and Abigail and June attack me with hugs, saying they can't wait for their little fritter.

Sue finds me after dinner. Dabbing her red eyes, she takes my hand and leads me over to the stairs away from everyone. She tucks my hair behind my ear. Now I know where her son gets it. "Thank you," she sniffs, struggling to hold herself together. "Thank you for coming into our lives, for loving us the way you do, and for making my son and the rest of us incredibly happy." She loses her grip and starts to cry as I reach for her hand, giving her a little squeeze. She takes a moment, getting a grip on herself. "I can't believe you're pregnant again."

I press my lips together, trying to hold myself together too. "I know. I'll be okay, Sue. Things are different this time around."

"I know, honey." She hugs me and wipes her cheeks. She walks me back into the living room, where Daniel wraps an arm around me, kissing my head.

"What's going on?" I ask, seeing Mark standing in front of a whiteboard he brought up from the office downstairs.

"Okay!" Mark calls, writing out the guys' names. "Who wants the first week in August?"

"I want the eleventh!" I announce, and Mark points his marker at me.

"Yes! Now we're talking. The baby mamma is on board!" He scribbles my name down. "What about the father?"

"The fourteenth," Cole calls out from behind me, wrapping his arms around my mid-section, "and I bet it's a girl."

"Ohhhh, this just got interesting!" Mark shouts. "Who's next?"

***

My fingers drum on the bar top. My phone is burning a hole in my pocket. It's been three and half months since Cole proposed to me, and two weeks since he left on his trip to Mexico. The trip is running smoothly. They've been gathering information on a client who's gone missing for the second time in the past three years. Washington has been using all their manpower trying to locate the man. They're not allowed to tell me who it is, and I'm not sure I want to know. However, it's been over five days since they were scheduled to return. I should know better than to worry, as they've been checking in twice a day, but something feels off.

I rub my stomach as Jake places my dinner in front of me. We didn't get a chance to eat this evening, as it was so busy, and we're both starving. We decide to eat at the bar since the evening is now slowing down.

The burger is delicious. I love how our cook knows about my love for mushrooms, as I've got lots piled under the bun. I load up part of my plate with mustard and ketchup, swirling it around to make the perfect combination. This baby likes some odd things.

"That's disgusting." Jake nearly gags on a fry.

I shrug and dip the mushroom burger into the blend, then biting off too big of a piece. "So good." I roll my eyes back, loving the tangy taste.

"Oh sweet Lord, that's..." Jake chucks his burger down on his plate, wiping his fingers clean. "I don't think we should eat together anymore." I laugh with a mouth full of food. "You're such a vision right now, Savi."

"Thanks." I down a glass of water to push the meat down faster. This baby is hungry!

Someone sits down, but I can't make out who it is, nor do I care. The burger is all I can focus on right now. Jake hands his plate to a server before he heads over to the customer.

"Hey, what can I get you tonight?"

"Actually, I need to see her." The voice makes me ill. His being here only means two things. He stands in front of me, while Jake comes to my side. "Could we have a moment alone, son?" He nods at Jake, who doesn't move.

"Jake stays." I push my plate away despite my stomach's protest. "What are you doing here, Frank?"

Frank shakes his head, not liking the extra set of ears, but he treads carefully. "I need you to come to Washington tomorrow. Lynn's case is up, and we need your testimony."

"And if I say no?" I counter, handing Gabe my plate as he stops to see who our guest is. "I'm not supposed to be put in stressful situations. If I got a doctor's note, would that help?"

Frank rubs his head. "Believe me, Savannah, I've tried to move mountains to get you out of this, but the court will subpoena you. You can either do it now, or later after the baby is born. My advice is get it over with now, so when that little tot comes, you can start fresh with all this behind you."

I pull out my phone and check for a possible missed call. "Does Cole know?" I want to cry out 'but he *promised,'* but I know I'm stronger than that. Frank shakes his head. I drop onto the lower counter, suddenly exhausted. "Who will be coming with me?"

"Who do you want?"

I want Keith, but he's out with the team.

"Mike?"

His face shows me he'd prefer Mike to stay running the house. "What about Sue?"

"Really?" I'm surprised by this.

"All right, I'll call Sue and let her know you agree." Frank stands, zipping his coat up. "Tomorrow, oh nine hundred hours, plan to be away for four days. And, Savannah, please don't run off this time." His eyes are not smiling.

I don't say anything; my nerves are already crawling to the surface.

Later that night as I crawl into my bed on the couch, I stare up at the ceiling and wonder what my father is doing right now. Is he with Lynn? Or is he staying away from her so as not to draw attention to their sick relationship? How on earth did I not know that the two of them were screwing behind my back? Am I that flipping naive? I let the events of the past run through my mind. I've been trying too hard to put this behind me, but it's not finished. I know it needs to be played out so I can be done with it once and for all. It doesn't make it any easier. I flop to the side, staring blankly at the TV that's playing the mini-series, The Hatfields and McCoys, on mute. The old movie makes so much sense. It's so cut and dry; you just take a gun and end the problem. Although if that were the case, I'd be dead long ago.

I chuck the blankets off and head to the bathroom for the fifth pee in the past thirty minutes. I haul my shirt up and look at my tummy in the mirror. I'm five and a half months and have a nice round bump forming. I think about how these last few months have gone. Cole has been wonderful, but his over-protectiveness is growing right along with the baby. It nearly killed him having to leave on this trip. I know he's been traveling a lot more lately to tie up as many cases as possible before little Sim comes.

The sound of the latch being unlocked on my door sends me to the living room, pressed against the wall in the shadow across from the door. My heart is pounding, but I know there are only three people who have a key. Jake, Keith, and Cole. A bag is tossed in first, followed by heavy footsteps. My fists clench as the dark figure is revealed, slumped with exhaustion, but the moment he spots me, his face lights up.

"I didn't mean to scare you." Cole closes the door behind him.

"It's okay," I whisper, staying where I am. He looks sexy in his army pants and jacket. His navy blue sweater peeks out the top of his scarf, making his eyes darker than normal, or he's just as excited to see me as I am him. He kicks off his boots and sheds his jacket.

"Come here," he commands with a dirty little twinkle in his eye. I step out from the wall and walk slowly toward him. His eyes drop to my favorite shirt. "Damn, baby, I love you in my clothes." His reaches out, touching my belly. "How's my little one behaving?"

"The little mite has an appetite." I place my hand over his. "Can't seem to get enough food."

"Can I get you anything?"

"Yes, but not food." I step back, pulling his shirt

over my head and tossing it to the couch. He runs his hand over his five o'clock shadow while he thinks about his next move. "Do you normally hesitate this much when you're in the field, Colonel?" I smirk, waiting for him to strike.

He smirks back at me. "This is different. I want to toss you up against the wall and hold you still while I work out the last two weeks of frustration on that tight little hole of yours, but," my chest falls heavily as my legs clench together, "I don't want to hurt you."

I roll my eyes as my sexual drive takes over. "Fine, I can find other ways that don't involve an over-protective fiancée. I have a showerhead with a multitude of settings." I turn on my heel but don't get three feet before he's behind me, bending me carefully over the kitchen table.

"Can your showerhead make you scream?" I hear his zipper, and his pants drop. I smile into the table, needing this so badly it hurts. His fingers explore how turned on I am, and they push in easily, pulling a moan from my chest. He bends his body over mine, kissing his way up my spine. "Spread your legs, baby." I do, and feel him brush my lust. He doesn't remove his fingers; he twists them around as I flex tightly onto him. "I needed you so badly I came right from North Dakota." His fingers slide out of me, and in slips his erection. "Oh god," he hisses. Starting a gentle flick of the hips, he rotates side to side, moving in all directions, raising my desire, my need, escalating my lust. His hands slide from my hips up to my shoulders. Once he has a firm grip, he presses me back into him. I scream his name, followed by a silent curse. "Don't ever question my need for you, Savannah." He grunts between each gentle but firm thrust. "I could snap you in two with the feelings that come over me when you're near." He pulls me up so I'm flat against his chest. His hands massage my breasts as he nips my neck. "Now I want you to come for me." His voice is a soft growl. "I need to feel you come, feel how much you missed me." He gently pushes me back over the table, lifts one of my legs so it's bent, and starts slowly thrusting hard and deep. His uncharacteristically measured, firm movements send me higher.

I claw, scream, and bite down as an orgasm rips through me. I can't see and can barely hear as I come back to myself. Cole carries my limp body to the bed, pulling the covers up.

"I need a shower." He kisses me roughly and disappears into the hallway.

His lazy smile remains imprinted on my brain as I drift off to a deep sleep.

***

Cole

Cole wraps the towel around his mid-section and peeks in on Savannah, who's passed out in the middle of the bed, her belly peeking out of the side of the blanket.

Her fridge is nearly empty, and her cabinets are pretty bare. What the hell has she been living on? Then he finds her stash. He grabs a spoon, and leaning against the counter, he scoops a huge ball of peanut butter into his mouth as his phone goes off in his coat pocket. He lunges for it, pressing the button before it can wake Savannah.

Frank: You made it there all right?

Cole: Yes, thanks for the heads up, Frank. I'll see you in Washington.

He thinks for a moment, then types.

Cole: What has she been eating these past two weeks?

Not even a moment later, he feels a vibration.

Jake: You don't even wanna know.

Cole: Try me.

Jake: You asked. Mustard-ketchup combo, mustard and potato chips, ketchup and potato chips. Oh! And her favorite right now is mustard, chips, and pickles all combined together. Your baby likes some f'd up foods, dude. I'm actually gagging right now.

Cole: Thanks for the visual. Appreciate it.

He changes quickly and heads outside.

***

"Savi," Cole whispers in her ear, but she doesn't move. "Baby, you need to get up." He kisses her cheek. "I have something you might like," he whispers, but still nothing. "I went to the market and got pickles and mustard." One of her eyes opens, and he grins. "I got all kinds of nasty food for you and Fritter."

"So we're back to Fritter?"

"Yes, it sounds cuter." She gives him an adorable smile. "Now, get up. There's a pile of pickles with your name on it."

"Really? Are you playing me?" She raises an eyebrow.

"No, I promise."

"How?"

"Jake." He squeezes her tight little bottom, enjoying the resulting moan.

"God, love a bestie who never sleeps." She stretches and rolls over, letting the sheet fall behind her. Her hand runs along her bare leg and up her side while she stares at him through those long lashes.

He tosses her a shirt. "As much as I want to roll around with you in this bed all day, you have a flight to catch in," he looks at her clock, "two hours."

Her face drops and she pulls the covers over her body again, not hiding from him, but from the idea of what's to come. He climbs in next to her, tucking her into his side.

"I know you're scared, but I'll be there with you every step of the way." She nods then slides off the bed, grabbing her robe and heading for the shower.

She stops at the last minute, her hand holding onto the doorframe for a beat, before she turns to look over her shoulder.

"I love you, Cole." She leaves before he can say anything.

***

On the drive to the airport and through the flight, Savannah is very quiet. Her fingers flip the pages to her book, *The Beach House* by James Patterson, but she's yet to open it. Cole understands her need for quiet and just keeps a firm grip on her thigh to comfort her. When they touch down in Washington, Frank is there to greet them at the gate, and he drives them directly to the base.

Frank's glance flickers to Savi's in the rear view mirror. "We're going to be briefing you on the case so you're up to speed on everything." He clears his throat when she doesn't respond, continuing to watch the countryside fly by. Cole reaches for her hand, but she doesn't turn. She tilts her head and traces a fallen raindrop on the glass. "So," Frank moves on, "after that, we'll have dinner and—"

"I want to speak to Lynn," she says softly, cutting him off. Cole feels the hairs on his neck raise. "Alone."

Frank's eyes jump to his. "Savannah, that's not something I can—"

"If you want me to testify," she turns for the first time to look directly at Frank, "you'll make it happen."

"Savannah…" Cole lowers his voice.

"Cole," she counters, and he realizes she's in a feisty mood right now. He reluctantly bites his tongue, pressing his back into the cool leather seat. She is closing herself off from them, he knows. She's most likely experiencing all the anger and hurt she has after so many years of loving this woman like a sister. He feels sick putting himself in her shoes. If Mark ever betrayed him like that, he'd be broken by it too. His hand finds its way to their baby, surprising hers, which is already there. He covers her hand, and she uses the other to wipe a tear. His body twitches to comfort her, but he knows she's on the brink of losing it.

Chapter Ten

Savannah

I feel like stone by the time I sit in an old chair with metal armrests across the table from four tired-looking lawyers. An older style clock ticks directly above the door, and my heart times its beat to its rhythm. Rain pelts at murky windows that look like they haven't been replaced since the early sixties. My nose tries to push the musty smell away, but it doesn't work, and it makes my stomach roll even more. My attention is pulled to one of the male lawyers. My gaze drops to a coffee stain on his tie, and I silently describe his appearance to try to help ground myself. He looks just like the man with the red stapler in the Office Space movie. I can tell he's hungry, as he keeps eyeing his partner's Snickers bar.

"Miss Miller," Morgan, the lead lawyer, says, pulling my attention to the present. She fusses with the paperwork in front of her. I remember this woman from the last time I was here. She's a perfectionist, and I want to lean over and mess up her meticulously lined up files and her pen sitting parallel. "I need you to understand that we can't have a repeat of what happened the last time you were in the court." She peers disapprovingly over the ridge of her glasses. My tongue presses to the roof of my mouth, trying like hell not to lash out at her. I hear Cole shift his body. I'm so tuned in to him, I know he wants to say something, but he won't…yet. "I understand it was hard for you, but—"

"Don't," I hiss in a small voice, but it's enough to shut her up for a moment.

"Miss Miller, if you want this testimony to count, you need to keep yourself calm. The judge will not tolerate an outburst. All it shows to the jury is that you're a loose cannon.""

"Is that why he got a double life sentence with no chance of parole?" I ask, cocking my head to the side. "Seems to me my outburst *and* the evidence proved to the jury that Denton is a monster, and he got what he deserved, so let's try this again, Miss Morgan." Her thumb starts clicking the top of her expensive pen. "I want five minutes alone with Lynn, before I testify against her tomorrow."

"That's not possible," she states.

I stand and grab my bag. Cole jumps to his feet. I expect him to try and stop me, but he doesn't.

"Wait," Morgan calls out, rubbing her head, "just sit for a moment."

I see Cole's mouth turn up, but when he turns around he's straight-faced again. God, he's good.

"It will take some time." One of the other

lawyers starts to argue, but she raises her bitchy hand, and he backs off.

"Morgan," the lawyer closest to Cole says, "they'll never go for it."

"Humphrey, when I want your input, I'll ask for it," Morgan snaps, rubbing her head harder. Humphrey flushes up his neck. *Poor guy.*

"Look," she closes her eyes, "give me an hour, and I'll see what I can do."

"Fine." I start to turn, but stop and lean back over the table, snatching the Snickers bar and placing it in front of her. "Just saying."

I see Humphrey cover his mouth, clearly getting my joke about the commercial. *'You're not yourself when you're hungry.'* Cole reaches for my arm and nearly pulls me out of the room. Once the door is closed, he bursts out laughing.

"I can't believe you did that," he croaks out. "Oh god, I wish Mark was here. He would have loved that." I smile, wishing he was too. His comic relief would be welcome right now. "Come on, let's get something to eat."

Two hours later, Humphrey is sent to find us in the cafeteria. He tells me after pulling in many favors, the judge still will not allow it, as Lynn has been violent since she's been in jail. I'm disappointed, but I get over it. I'll see her tomorrow, and I'll get to say my piece then, with or without the judge's help.

We head back up to that horrible room and spend the next several hours getting briefed. I must say Morgan is a little nicer this time around. Guess the Snickers bar worked.

The briefing lasts till evening, and we go down to the restaurant.

I stay lost in my thoughts throughout dinner. The guys try to engage me, but I am off in childhood memories with Lynn.

"Merry Christmas, Lynnie."I hold out a little white box and grin.

She snatches it out of my hand, ripping the bow in two. "Aww." She pulls out a chain with a half of a jagged heart dangling from the center. Lynn loves hearts.

"See?" I pull the other half out from under my shirt. "Not just friends—"

"But sisters too," she finishes, admiring the necklace in the mirror. "Love you, Savi."

"Love you too, Lynnie."

I keep trying to pinpoint the spot when she turned on me. It's a deep ache that burns in my stomach when I think about her. How can someone imprint so strongly on your life one moment, and the next hire someone to kill you? I feel like I'm in a movie. Did our time together mean nothing to her? Surely there's got to be a time when she loved me like the sister I felt she was, the way I did her.

I can't eat, and I don't touch my water. I'm so lost I hardly feel Cole help me out of my chair and walk us upstairs to our hotel room. He lets me know he and Frank have some more to discuss, so he'll be in the other room, and suggests I take a bath.

"Then get some sleep, baby." He leans in, kissing my lips and giving my belly a rub. I nod, sitting on the couch staring at a black screen that stares back at me.

***

"Do you solemnly affirm that you will tell the truth, the whole truth, and nothing but the truth?" The clerk stares with piercing gray eyes, and a chill runs up my spine.

"I do," I say weakly, feeling my voice run like hell in the opposite direction. I felt more confident when I testified against Denton, but Lynn…I sit a little straighter and glance at the jury. Nine men, three women, one wearing a horrendous cat sweater she must have made herself, because no one in their right mind would try and market it.

Cole catches my eye and gives me a little wink, letting me know he's only fifteen steps away. I nod, swallow hard, and try to keep myself together. Cole's words repeat over and over in my head. "Just one more day, baby, then we can go home and put all this behind us." A door opens and a light roar of whispers erupts. I keep my eyes locked on Cole's, suddenly terrified to look over and face my reality. He mouths, "I love you." I barely nod and tune in to the judge, who is handing the floor over to Lynn's lawyer.

I'm shaking. I'm not ready. I'm so scared.

I force my eyes over to face my once best friend, my sister, and now my enemy who might get life…if she's lucky.

Lynn's face is paler than normal, and she's dressed to play the part of the young, innocent woman. She's wearing a cream colored skirt that hits right above the knee, white blouse, and a baby pink sweater, something Lynn would *never* wear.

Hell, even her hair is down and pinned straight, and she hates her hair that way. I don't fall for it, of course. I know her, and I see it's still her in there. I do recognize her body language, right down to how she shifts in that cotton blouse. She hates cotton; Lynn always wears silk. Seeing her obvious attempt to hide her real self lights a small spark deep inside me. Though I do see her wrist is in a brace, and there's some dark color around an eye. I guess she has been fighting.

Her head lifts up and her eyes lock onto mine. A series of emotions run through me, but suddenly the strongest is pity. Not the kind of pity where I wish she weren't sitting there waiting for her fate to be determined, but the kind where I know she'll never have a life to call her own. *Karma.*

I think she misreads my look and gives me a tiny smile and mouths, "Hi, honey."

I sink my teeth into my cheek to the point of pain, but I let go when the lawyer clears his throat.

"Shall I repeat my question?"

I nod and give him my attention. "How long have you and Lynn been friends?"

"Since…" I cough, begging my voice to return. "Since we were tiny."

"Would you say she's like a sister?" My lawyer interrupts, but the judge waves him off.

"Yes."

"You two did everything together?"

"Yes."

"Family trips?"

"Yes." I shrug.

"Family dinners—"

His voice trails off into nothing when my mind recalls one particular family dinner. I'm sucked into a flashback and the courtroom fades…

…to my father's penthouse, where I'm showing up early because traffic was light, as so many people are out of the city for Thanksgiving. I open the door to see the place looks empty, but the smell of turkey makes my stomach jump to attention. Chucking my purse down next to another one, at the time I don't notice, but now I see it's hers. The cook is busy in the kitchen, so I leave him be.

"Dad?" I call out, removing my shoes from my aching feet. "You here yet?"

I scramble up the twisty stairs to the second floor, and come face to face with my flushed father. "Hey, Dad." I grin, but it fades when I see the panicked look on his face. "Everything all right?"

He pulls my arm and pushes me in front of him, hurrying me down the stairs toward the front door. "Can we re-schedule, dear? Something has come up. I'm sorry, but it can't be helped."

"What?" I pull my arm free, only to have him snatch it up again. "But it's Thanksgiving. What about dinner?"

"Savannah, you're twenty-two years old. Don't you think it's about time you find someone else to spend it with?"

My face snaps back. "Wow! You know, some fathers would kill to have their daughter spend special occasions with them."

He opens the door and shoves my purse in my hands. "I'll call you later." And with that, the door is slammed in my face.

"What the hell was that?" I curse, pulling out my phone as I hurry to the elevator. Once I'm outside, I call Lynn, planning to warn her not to head to Dad's, since he's being an ass again. It goes straight to voice mail. I try again, knowing she'll pick up if I call right after.

"Hello?" Lynn's muffled voice comes over the line.

"Hey, Lynn. Shit, Dad's in another damn mood, so I'd suggest—" "Shhh, it's Savi," I hear her whisper to someone.

I grin. "Lynn, you're not alone? Where are you?"

"I-I'm at home. I-I was just about to leave, so I'm glad you called." I plug one ear as a firetruck goes by.

"Shit, Savi, ahh…my landlady is here again, so you know what that means."

"Yeah, have fun with that."

The vision fades away, and I'm back in the courtroom. The lawyer is prattling on about something, but I ignore him. I look back over at Lynn. The room feels as if the air is slowly being sucked out through a straw, causing my lungs to shrivel up and turn to dust. I realize what an idiot I was not noticing her purse, and now realizing I could hear that firetruck through her phone in the distance.

"You bitch," I snarl at her. She tilts her head, trying to understand where I'm coming from.

"What was that, Miss Miller?" her lawyer asks, raising a thick eyebrow at me.

"Yes, Lynn attended almost all family events,

even some she and my father made up together." I watch her face fall and the color drain from it.

"How close would you say she was with your father?"

I shake my head while staring at her. She looks panicky, and I realize this is something that hasn't come out yet. "Is sleeping with my father at twenty-two close enough?" Her face lowers forward into her hands, drawing the jurors' attention to her. The courtroom suddenly grows loud, and the judge bangs his gavel repeatedly. Once the room settles, the lawyer starts in on me again but never touches on that topic.

***

I've been in the witness seat now for an hour and a half, and I'm growing tired. I know I'm stressed, because I think I'm getting small Braxton Hicks contractions. Dr. Brown warned me this could happen, so I'm not too concerned. Our lawyer has asked for a recess, seeing my discomfort, but I refused. I just want this to be finished. When I walk out those doors, I'm not coming back in.

Cole is watching me like a hawk. I can see he's worried; he keeps rubbing his face and twitching. I try to nod and let him know I'm fine, but really I'm growing more and more finished with rehashing my life to complete strangers who are judging my every word.

"Miss Miller," the lawyer mutters, heading back to his table and making a dramatic effect as he thinks, "do you love your father?" I start to answer, but he cuts me off.

"Remember, you are under oath."

I think about my words to be sure they're the right ones. "Yes, I love my father, but when he got into politics…"

"So now you don't?" he snaps quickly

"Would you?" I snap back, hurt.

"I'm not on the witness stand." I swear he smirks momentarily.

"My father doesn't want me, and I don't want him. It's simple, and I've come to terms with it." I rub my aching tummy.

He nods, pacing in front of me. "So you get 'rescued,' stay in a safe house, fall in love, get pregnant, all in a very short time? No offense, Miss Miller, but that doesn't make you look like you're a grieving victim." I lock my jaw, but my tongue is battling to be let loose. "What I see," he turns to address the jurors, "is a rich, bored little girl who hatched this plan and didn't care who she took down. Should we be looking into the Colonel to see if he was involved too?" I know he's trying to get me to break and let fly at him. I won't lie, I'm frigging close. I grab my stomach and blink wildly. "Just tell me why. Why hatch such a lie to take down everyone in your family, and especially this woman who was like a sister to you?" I run my sweaty hand over my mouth. "What has she ever done to you?"

I need to get out of here.

"Please," I whisper, but he keeps talking. "Please." I heave forward.

"Stop!" Lynn calls out and the whole room

stops. "Savi?"

I think I'm going to be sick because she's trying to show concern for me. I shake my head at her. "Don't you dare!" I'm nearly in tears now. "You sat across from me in a room while I was being held hostage and didn't shed a tear for me when I begged you to let me go." I point my finger at her face. "You *sat* across the table from me while my father shot my friend in the face! Don't you dare try to pretend you care now!"

"The jury will disregard that last comment," the judge orders. Every member on that jury is staring at me with concern and interest.

"You screwed your way up the political ladder," I continue firmly but loudly, "and for what, Lynn? A cell block, a roommate, and shitty food?" The judge is yelling, but I don't care, raising my voice louder. "You may have taken my life from me, but I found a hell of a lot better one. You're pathetic. I feel nothing but pity for you!"

"Order! Recess!" The judge bangs his gavel loudly. The clerk helps me up and I hold the bottom of my stomach. Cole rushes to my side, wrapping a protective arm around my waist and yelling at Morgan that I'm done, no more. They got what they needed from me.

Once we round the corner and are away from the rush of people, Cole turns to check me over. His hands are everywhere. "Are you all right? What can I do? Should I call the doctor?" His words are frantic until he sees my face. "Why are you smiling?"

"Just call me a good actor." I shrug.

"You're not hurting?" He looks a little pissed.

"No, I am, but I knew we'd have to break soon, and there's no way I'm going back into that room. So I did what I had to, to make sure I got to tell Lynn what I wanted to say."

"Which was?"

"Which is no matter what, I'm still coming out of this on top." I pull him into me, resting my head on his shoulder. "I didn't mean to scare you, but I needed this to be over."

His hand wraps around my hair and tugs my head backward to look at him. "I couldn't handle sitting there for too much longer anyway." He kisses my lips and takes my hand. "Come on, let's see if we can get an early flight back home."

***

Frank shakes his head at me and smiles. "I guess it could have been worse." He holds the car door open for me. "Thanks for not getting held in contempt this time."

"No problem," I joke, settling into my seat and feeling a mixture of things. I know it will take some time to work things out, but now this chapter can be closed, at least for me.

Cole settles in next to me, placing his warm hand on my leg. Suddenly, my hormones kick in full throttle. I casually slip my hand on his thigh, dipping low and feeling him immediately spring to attention. He shakes his head, laughing under his breath.

"You're killing me, baby." He leans down and

gives me a quick kiss, pulling back slightly with his mouth hovering near my lips. "Oh, the things I'd do to you if we were alone."

My body hums with excitement. "Oh, the things I'd let you do to me if we were alone." I bite my bottom lip playfully.

"Frank, get out," he jokes as we pull into traffic. Poor Frank just shakes his head and turns up the radio.

"I love you, Cole," I whisper, nuzzling into his neck and seeking his comfort.

"Is that so?"

I kiss my favorite spot along his jawline. "It is." I doze off, and savor the fact that I'm finished with my part of the court proceedings.

I manage to get a little sleep on the plane as Cole rubs soothing circles over our little Fritter, relaxing my sore muscles as I think about my mother and what she'd think about this entire situation. The only upside to her not being here is she can't be affected by any of this. I only hope she can see I love someone who loves me as much I do him.

I wiggle my fingers, moving the heavy diamond and relishing its feeling and what it represents. Cole lifts my hand to his mouth and kisses the ring; he is so tuned to my thoughts.

"Cole?" I turn to look up at him. "I want to go home."

"That's where we're headed." He brushes my hair off my face.

"No," I shake my head, "I want to come home."

His eyes sparkle as his finger traces along my brow, down my cheekbone, and stops at my lips.

"Yeah, baby, let's go home." He leans down, sealing his mouth over mine and our words into a promise. I doze off, comforted by the warmth of his hand on my thigh.

The North Dakota airport is quiet. There are very few people around, as it's the middle of the night. I'm not looking forward to the long drive home, but I know I won't have to return to Washington for a very long time. If ever.

As we step outside into the fresh air, my fingers slip on the strap and I drop my bag, tripping over it and nearly falling flat on my face. Cole catches me in time and tugs me close to him. He checks me over, hands everywhere. I bat them away and tell him to stop fussing. I laugh when he starts in harder, clearly making fun of the situation. He suddenly pulls me in for a kiss, chuckling while his tongue plays with mine. A gust of wind whips my hair wildly around my face.

We both freeze as we hear *his* voice.

Chapter Eleven

"Savannah." A chill rips through me, tearing a hole in my armor and turning me into a quivering mass. My senses lock onto the 40mm pointed directly at me.

Though his face is shaded by a hat, I see sweat dripping from his brow. A drop lands on his lip then is blown away by his rapid breathing. At first glance, he looks all business. One wouldn't think he'd be carrying a weapon into an airport. I now know his look, and this will end in one of two ways. *Either one, I lose.*

Everything grows quiet, even though chaos whirls on around us. Time seems to stand still. I can only hear the mad beating of my own heart. I should have known better than to think I could ever be truly free. In slow motion, I look to Cole and say a silent goodbye. I want to cry, but I can't seem to find the emotion. It's lost like the rest of my life. "I love you," I mouth.

The gun is steady. He has complete control, and his eyes have never left my face.

Suddenly, Keith and Mark both appear out of nowhere, weapons drawn.

"No," Cole whispers. His grip tightens around my fingers.

The gun lowers to my stomach before he speaks. "The one woman I truly loved, you took from me. You have always been in the way. Enough is enough, Savannah." His bitter words cut through me.

Mark shifts closer to my side, muttering something to Cole, but I can't understand them.

"Dad?" I try to sound in control. I pull my hand out of Cole's death grip. I have no idea what to say, so I go with the first thing that comes to mind. "Can I ask you one thing, please?" I take a shaky step forward. The hot, heavy tears pooling in my eyes blur my vision. I hear the sound of guns shifting in the hands of those who are now surrounding us. "Do you remember the year we went up to northern Canada for Christmas? The year before Mom found out she was sick?" He nods, clearly annoyed by this trip down memory lane. "It was around eight at night when the power went out."

"Six," he corrects me, flipping the gun for me to hurry up.

"The temperature dropped, and we all huddled by the fire, not caring because we had our tree, the heat, and hot chocolate."

He rubs his head and mutters, "What's your point?"

I swallow hard, forcing my emotions back and taking another step closer. Where this bravery is coming from, I don't know. Maybe my mother is here, or maybe I'm just losing it.

"Savannah, stop," Cole warns behind me, but I hear him tell the other men to stand back too.

The gun is closer now. I can smell the steel. "Did you love me then?" I hold his gaze and see a tiny flicker in his eyes. His gun wavers a bit, then he points it directly in my face and pulls the trigger.

No.

Pop! Pop! Pop! I'm blinded and falling hard. The breath is knocked out of me as I'm covered with heavy bodies.

***

I wake to semi-darkness. It takes me a moment to see I'm in Cole's bed, and he's standing in front of the fireplace watching the flames and sipping brandy. He's only in a pair of pajama pants, his bare chest reflecting orange from the fire. He looks so tall and powerful the way his muscles flex, casting shadows. His head presses into his hand gripping the mantel.

I slip out of bed, move behind him, and run my hands along his warm back, feeling him jump then immediately relax. "Hey," I whisper against his skin, giving him a little kiss, "everything all right?"

"No," he mutters, downing the rest of his brandy. He puts the glass on the mantel and turns in one swift movement to face me, holding my head in his hands. His eyes are dark; I can see he's fighting to hold himself together. One hand moves to my hair, entangling his fingers and getting a good grip, while he leans forward and rests his forehead to mine, squeezing his eyes shut. "I can't do this again. I can't have you leave me. I need you, Savannah. I need you to be mine." His words seem painful.

"I am yours," I whisper.

His eyes suddenly pop open.

"Marry me now."

"Now? Cole, it's the middle of the night."

"Then tomorrow." He sounds frantic. "I promise I'll give you a fancy wedding later, just marry me."

I lean forward and press my hands over his chest. "Cole, I love you more than the earth needs the sun, but nothing in my life has ever been in my control. *Ever.* I want to stress about the food, the flowers, and the music, all that ridiculous wedding stuff. Because it will be normal—*my normal*—and I need normal." I walk my fingers up his chest. "Please understand how much I need this, how much I want it."

I can see his internal battle flickering though his eyes. His tongue runs over his bottom lip, the moisture on them catching the flicker of the flames.

"If stressing over food, flowers, and music makes you get your normal, then I'll wait," he says quietly. I'm pleased he hears me, but I can see something is still weighing on him.

I start to say more, but he picks me up, laying me back down on the bed. I think he's going to kiss me, but instead he lies down next to me, resting his head on my chest, his hand on my tummy. We stay like that for a long time, my fingers combing through his dark, silky hair. The only noise is the soothing sound of the fire. Just as I'm about to fall asleep, he speaks in a quiet, raspy voice.

"Tonight did things to me, Savannah." He draws a small square pattern along my belly. "Even though we got him, he did pull the trigger." He clears his throat. "Images flash before my eyes." Blinking away tears, I still can't believe my father pulled a gun on me, let alone actually pulled the trigger. I know why he did it, I know why the gun wasn't loaded. He was too much of a coward to kill himself, so he made others do it. If he had really wanted to kill me, he'd never do it at an airport with so much security around. My father is—was—a selfish, dangerous man who never thought of anyone but himself. "I've always been in control of my life," Cole continues. "Since I've met you, though, I've been tested. I need it to feel right again, so bear with me, because I'm going to be an over-protective husband and father. Give me time to work through these issues, all right?"

I lean down, kissing his hair like he always does mine. "I understand."

He kisses my belly then shifts so he's up on his pillow. "I need to hold you." I roll into him, tucking my head under his neck. I can feel his body battling with itself to work through what he witnessed tonight.

"Cole?"

"Mmm," he answers like he's a million miles away.

"How did my father find us at the airport?"

He waits a beat. "Mark checked with the airline. Looks like he followed us from the courthouse. He was on the same plane."

"How did he get a gun through security?"

Cole shakes his head. "They have footage of him retrieving it from a locker. He paid someone to leave it there. Mark found the man. He's just some lowlife looking to make a quick buck. He's been arrested, and he'll get a little time."

"Oh." I shudder, pushing the thought out of my head. He's gone, and that's all that matters now.

"You're safe now, baby." He pulls me tighter, lowering his voice and lacing it with a dark undertone. "No one will ever hurt you again. I promise you that."

I don't doubt his words, and for once I allow myself to believe I'm going to be okay. I keep quiet after that, falling asleep to the even sounds of his heartbeat.

Chapter Twelve

Cole

Cole tries to hold back a smile. "Steak or chicken?" she asks, holding up both packages. Her tanned belly is peeking out the bottom of her tank top. Her eyes narrow in on him. *Shit*. "Don't even, Cole."

He holds up his hands, but a smile breaks through. She's so damn sweet. Before he can blink, she's tossing a bag of chips at him. He laughs, catching them mid-toss.

"I'm sorry." He heads toward her and snags her around the waist. "You're the prettiest pregnant woman in here." He nuzzles her neck and breathes in her scent. Everything comes alive when that smell hits him, sending messages to the part she owns deep within him, the very middle of his heart.

She flinches suddenly, and his training kicks in. His eyes snap up, quickly tuning in to their surroundings.

"Cole," she whispers, her body stiff as a board.

"Ummm."

He pulls back and sees her face growing pale, but her eyes are telling a different story. They are soft and growing excited.

"Cole, my water broke!"

He drops his eyes to the tiny line of water trickling down her leg, pooling by her pink toes. He quickly pulls out his cell phone. "Mark, it's time." She grins when she hears Mark hoot in the phone. Her teeth pull in her bottom lip; she's nervous. "Okay, baby." He takes her hand to help her step around her little puddle. "Let's get you to the car."

"Okay." She rubs her stomach and closes her eyes briefly, no doubt calming herself.

He hooks his arm around her back and under her knees, lifting her into the SUV. She suddenly holds her stomach, squeezing her eyes shut.

"Oh, oww," she cries, taking short breaths.

Cole pulls out his cell, starting the stopwatch. After buckling her in, he runs to the driver's seat and starts the car, turning the fan up to blow cool air on her damp skin.

By the time they reach the hospital, her contractions are ten minutes apart. They get her registered and in a room before Cole allows himself to relax a little, though he'd never let Savannah know he's nervous. Good Lord, what if something goes wrong? He scrubs his hands over his face as he lets out a long, bottom-of-the-lung sigh.

"Twenty bucks for your thoughts?" Mark walks up the hall toward Cole. Cole shrugs off his jitters and nods at the man he will always consider his brother. "How is she holding up?"

"Good." He takes the coffee Mark hands him. "They need to do another exam. I just wanted to give her some privacy." He shakes his head, chasing away the images from his head. "There's a lot of people…down there." He makes an action with his hands. "I thought I might murder someone." He rubs his hand over his scalp. "I just want her, *them*, to be okay."

Mark's hand lands heavily on his shoulder, giving it a tight squeeze, "Savi's a fighter, and it stands to reason that little spitfire in there will be a fighter too, just like Mama." He grins, making Cole feel like he's got a whole extra set of balls right now. "Besides, you think any of those doctors would piss off the Green Beret in the delivery room?"

Cole laughs, letting the tension go.

"Excuse me, Daddy?" A nurse peeks her head out the door. She looks like a pixie. "It's time."

"Go make me an uncle." Mark smacks his shoulder. "Seriously, give Savi a kiss for me."

"Yeah." Cole finds himself grinning. *Holy shit*, I'm gonna to be a dad.

The clock reads seven, and they've been at this for five hours. Savannah's exhausted, Cole is beyond beat, which is odd because he can usually be up for sixty some-odd hours and still have no problem functioning. But this…this is different, this is his love and his child. His mind slips away momentarily.

Mark glances at Cole through the garage window. The corner of his right eye is bleeding, his lip is cracked, and his arm hangs loose. Cole watches as Mark's mother grabs a chair and lifts it above her head. He lunges forward, kicking in the window, but by the time his eyes adjust, he sees Mark unconscious on the floor. His mother smashed a chair over her own son. A mother. It's disgusting. Cole pushes her out of the way and drops to his knees, feeling around Mark's body. Please be okay!

"Cole, Cole?" Savannah's voice pulls him from the memory. "Could you hand me some ice water?"

He nods, promising himself that his child will never go through anything like what Mark had to endure.

"Okay, Savannah, I know this has been exhausting for you, but we need to do a C-section. You can't pass her shoulders, and she is lodged in there pretty tight." Dr. Brown looks over at Cole, and he feels the blood drain from his face. "It's routine, and it's actually less stress on the baby."

Savi reaches for his hand and gives it a hard squeeze. He pushes aside all his own fear as he looks down at her scared eyes.

"Less stress for the baby and no more pushing sounds like a good plan to me." He leans down, kissing her lips. "I'll be right there with you the whole time, my love."

"Okay," she sighs, her voice so weak with exhaustion that she barely gets the single word out. "Let's do this."

Dr. Brown nods at Cole. "Okay, Dad, you go with the nurse and put on some scrubs. Savannah, we need to get you all set up for the anesthesiologist."

After thirty agonizing minutes of pacing outside

the room, Dr. Brown calls Cole to come in. Savannah is lying on a table, arms strapped down, and a sheet is blocking her view of what is happening.

"Hi, baby." He moves into her view, grinning behind his mask.

"I feel funny." She grins, but he notices her whole body is shaking. He looks over at a doctor sitting next to her head.

"All normal. Some people get the shakes, some people get the shivers." The doctor extends his hand. "Dr. Melnik. I'm the anesthesiologist and an OBG as well. She's in great hands here."

"Cole Logan, the father. That's great to hear."

"Savannah?" Dr. Brown says over the sheet divider. "Tell me if you can feel this." Cole peeks over and sees the doctor poke the bottom of her belly.

"No." Her voice is shaky.

"Perfect." Dr. Brown grins at Cole but doesn't warn him when she makes the first cut.

Oh Lord! His knees buckle, but he senses Savannah is watching him, so he pulls it together…somewhat. Her eyes lock onto his, showing terror and excitement all at once.

"You will feel some pressure," Dr. Brown announces, and suddenly Savannah is being moved about, but she doesn't seem to notice too much.

Something tells him to look, and before his brain can catch up, he glances over and sees his daughter as she is pulled from her mother's womb.

Air, movement, chatter, heartbeat, everything stops when his eyes land on his little girl.

"Oh my god!" he whispers in awe.

"No matter what," Savannah makes him look down at her, "you don't leave her side. Promise me, Cole."

"I promise."

Savannah's chin starts to quiver, and she bursts into tears when she hears their baby cry for the first time. Cole has to agree, it's the best sound in the entire world.

He kisses her hand. "I'll be right back." He steps up next to the nurse, who is cleaning the baby's skin and clearing her lungs. She's crying hard, and his hands itch to scoop her up. He bites his cheek. He wants to yell at the nurse to be careful. Lord, she's only seconds old! *Let me hold her, damn it!* His blood pressure is through the roof, and he's sweating from the damn full body outfit they have him in. All he wants is…

"Here you go, Daddy." The nurse turns, holding his daughter bundled up like a burrito. "Seven pounds, one ounce, and she has a great set of lungs on her." She places her in his arms.

As soon as she's nuzzled up next to his chest, she immediately stops crying. Her little black eyes open and stare at him. Tiny pink lips just like her mother's latch onto her fist, and she starts to suck.

She's perfect.

"Hi," he whispers, feeling tears slip out of his eyes. "I'm your daddy." He raises her to his face and breathes in her smell, embedding it in his memory. "Let's go see Mommy."

Savannah cries again when he holds her out close to her chest. Her arms are still strapped down, so he lifts her up to her face, letting her have skin to skin contact.

"Hi, baby girl." Savi smiles. "Oh! She has your eyes, Cole."

Cole grins, thinking everything about their baby is Savannah. That's why she's perfect.

After a rather rough bath, *so Cole thought*, finger and footprints are done, and everything that can be measured and poked is complete, and he *finally* gets to hold her again. He's told to hang out in the room in a rocking chair to wait until Savannah is moved to her room.

The wooden rocking chair has a soothing creak to it, and soon he finds a rhythm she enjoys and they both settle in.

Her little hands are free, and one is jammed in her mouth, making the cutest sucking noise. The other rubs his shirt back and forth. He sticks his finger into her palm, and she quickly latches on, making an adorable coo sound. This breaks the dam, and he starts to cry. He's emotionally exhausted, something that never happened until Savannah came into his life.

"You have some guests." The nurse points to a viewing window.

Cole carefully stands and brings her over to the window where his mother, Abigail, and June are pressed against the glass. He laughs as they all melt over her.

"Oh, sweet one, you are going to be so loved," he whispers into her tiny ear. "Mostly by your mother and me." Her dark eyes peek up at him, almost like she understands. "Daddy's little girl, aren't ya?" She makes a tiny squeak, making his heart squeeze.

Savannah is staring out the window when he returns to her room. She looks beat, but when she spots them coming in, her face lights up.

"How is she?" she whispers, holding out her arms.

"Perfect, of course." Cole waits for the nurse to park the rolling cot next to Savi, then places her in her eager arms.

"Oh," she sniffs, "hello, my little girl."

Cole sits so he's next to them, wrapping his arm around her back. He holds out his finger to the baby, pressing it back into her grasp and loving the bond they already have.

Savannah looks up at him, showing him her beautiful face. "We did it, Cole. We made it to the other side. We're going to be okay now."

Cole kisses her shoulder and looks at his little family. "Yeah, baby, we're going to be just fine."

She beams, relaxing against him.

"Savi?" he whispers, "I think I have the perfect name for her."

"Oh?"

He leans in and whispers. She suddenly turns into his shoulder and breaks into another sob. He knows they are happy tears. It's the perfect name for her…the perfect name to remember.

***

Savannah

I head to the kitchen to retrieve a bottle of water. The morning walks Abigail and I have been taking make my body feel like it's mine again.

I tap the counter, debating do it, or don't? It's just sitting there taunting me, calling me to use it. I never have before, but it's the only way to find him on this massive property. My fingers twitch then retract. Come on, Savi, do it. *Fine*! I pick up the radio, turning it to channel seven.

"Keith?"

"Savannah?" His voice is confused. "Are you all right?"

"Yes, umm…can I see you?"

"Yeah, I'm outside by the stables."

The sun is hot, *finally*, making my face flush as I walk down the pebble path. My long skirt hugs my legs as a breeze swirls around me. My hair blinds me momentarily, as my nose detects a heavenly scent. I love the mountains. Everything feels so fresh and natural. No city smog to ruin the crisp air. No car horns or buses, just nature.

I find Keith fixing the gate, but stop to laugh when I see one of the horses nuzzling his pocket. He keeps grumbling at her to move it along. Finally, he gives up and turns to pat her nose. "You're needy today, Winnie. I don't have time to play." I rest my arms over the rail and watch. The black pony, Winnie, nips at his pocket again. "Really?" He sighs. "Fine, but don't tell anyone." He pulls out a half-eaten peanut bar and holds it to her mouth.

"I saw that." I grin and duck under the rail,

heading toward them.

"She wouldn't leave me alone." He shrugs, acting like it was nothing.

"Whatever, softy, your secret is safe with me."

He rolls eyes and grabs a hammer. "So, what's up?" I dig my sandal into the dirt and think about how to start this conversation. Keith and I are close, but this is a big deal. He turns to look at me, since I haven't said anything for the past fifteen seconds. "What's the problem?"

"The wedding is in, ah…two weeks." I stumble over my words. "I, umm, I've been thinking."

He closes his eyes. "You don't have cold feet, do you?"

"No!" I laugh. "God, no." I sigh and move closer to him. "I don't have any family left—from, you know—my side. You are the one I'm closest too, the one I consider my big brother." He sets the hammer down and turns his attention on me. *Screw it*. "Keith, will you walk me down the aisle?"

His face changes as my words sink in, and his eyes soften then gloss over. "It would be my honor, Savannah." I leap into his arms, and he gasps at the force. "Thank you, Keith, so, so much." He hugs me hard before he clears his throat and steps back.

"Right, well, you tell me when and where, and I'll show up." I shake my head at his comment. *Men.*

I step back but smirk. "You better."

"Wouldn't miss it for the world." He grabs his hammer and heads back to the gate. I turn on my heel, feeling so pleased at our conversation.

"Savannah?"

"Yeah?"

"Thank you."

***

"Wow," I whisper in the mirror. I hardly recognize myself. "Molly, you did an amazing job." My makeup is flawless, and my hair hangs in long curls with one side pinned up.

"Here we are." Abigail beams, holding my garment bag. She hooks it behind the privacy divider. "Would you like anything?"

"Mark wanted you to have this." June hands me a martini. "It will help with the nerves."

Oh, I love Mark.

"Hand it over," I say, then take a long sip. I'm not nervous about getting married, just the thought of standing in front of everyone gives me the jitters. Thankfully, we kept it to a small number, not that a hundred and fifty is small.

Sue gasps when I step out to show them my dress.

"Holy…" I jump at the sound of John's voice from the doorway. "Sorry, but you look great, Savannah."

I look down at the form-fitting white dress that hugs my curves. A slit stops at mid-thigh. The beading starts at the right hip, spreading up and across to my left shoulder and scattering up the halter strap. It's the only piece of New York I would allow on this day. Sue called in a favor from a friend when she got word about the dress I wanted. Four weeks later, I found it hanging in my old closet with a note.

Your mother would have gotten it for you. I just helped her.
~ Sue

Needless to say, I sobbed.

"Sue," John motions with his head, "Zack is here with his crew to set up the food. Would you show him where to go?"

"Yes, of course." She turns to me. "It's perfect, honey." I lean in and give her a kiss on the cheek.

"Thank you, Sue."

June appears from somewhere with a secret little smile. "Here." She opens a velvet bag and pulls out a deep red garter outlined with black lace. "A little something for later."

I laugh as she pushes my dress back, slipping the garter over my shoe and up my leg, just above where the slit in my skirt stops.

"I love it." I wrap my arms around her, thinking this day couldn't get any better.

"Okay," June starts to fan her eyes, "I need to grab my camera. I'll see you down there."

I move toward to the mirror, taking one last look at myself. I start to feel a little emotional. I would sell my soul to have my mother here with me today. The more I look, the more I see her in me.

"All right, ladies, the show is about—" Keith stops at the door. I catch his reflection in the mirror. His mouth drops open. "You look very pretty, Savannah." I smile and press my lips together. He stands a little straighter then steps forward, offering me an arm. "Miss Miller, it is time."

I thread my arm through his and take a deep breath. "Don't let me trip."

"Never." He grins down at me. "Come on, your future waits downstairs."

This is our day, our moment, our time. I beam up at Keith, feeling complete.

"Okay, I'm ready."

Chapter Thirteen

Sue and Daniel have outdone themselves with decorating the entire house and grounds for our outdoor wedding. Yellow roses line the walkway leading outside to the rows and rows of chairs full of eager people patiently waiting for my arrival.

I hear Abigail scold Mark for dipping into the appetizers. I chuckle and think that only Mark would hold things up at our wedding because he's sneaking food. Bottomless pit.

I hear her behind me, and the warmth that spreads right down to my toes is worth the possible spit-up that comes along with that sound. I whirl around and see her dark eyes peeking out from her tiny white hat. "Hellooo, my little love." I lift my daughter out of Sue's arms, cradling her in mine, breathing in her scent. She warms my heart from the inside out. "Are you going to behave for Mommy and Daddy today?"

"Fat chance." Mark grins and gives me a kiss on the cheek. "She is, after all, half you," he jokes, then steps back to take in my dress. "Oh, Cole is gonna love this."

"Mark!" Abigail hisses from the doorway. "Go."

"I am, I am," he mutters, heading outside. "Relax!"

"Come here, Olivia." Sue holds out her hands, taking her from me. I feel my heart squeeze when I hear her name. My mother's name. "Come on, Grandpa," Sue calls. "You and I need to help this little thing throw some flower petals. Let's make a mess!" She throws some in the air, laughing and hugging Olivia to her. It's hard to believe she's already six weeks old. "Let's not make Daddy anxious by keeping him waiting, or he'll get Uncle Keith to stick a tracking device on you." Sue laughs at Keith, who gives a nod with a deadpan expression.

"Savannah," Daniel grasps my elbow and leans down to whisper in my ear. "I wanted to give you my gift now. Lynn got life without parole."

I lean back to look at him. "Really?"

"Yes," his face lights up as his news sinks in. The fact that I'm not overly saddened by this makes me see I've made progress. My past is behind me. I give a little smile and know I'll be all right.

"Now," he gives me a kiss on the cheek, "it's your turn to live." I wrap my arms around his waist and mutter a heartfelt thank you.

"Have no fear, your Male of Honor is here." Jake comes strolling in, looking like he jumped out of a tuxedo ad. "I'm ready when you are."

"You're late." I raise an eyebrow.

"Sorry." He blushes, and I don't even want to know. Graham slips through the door, not making eye contact. I smack Jake's arm and roll my eyes.

"Really?"

"He surprised me with a trip to L.A." He shrugs, but I see his excitement just below the surface. "We're going to be staying with his cousin, Pete. It's getting serrriiious." I give him a hug. I know how important Graham is to him.

"I'm so happy for you, Jake, I am."

Suddenly, the music starts, which brings on the butterflies. *This is it.* Keith hooks my arm and nudges me forward.

"You're up, sweetheart." He smiles down at me. Jake walks behind Sue and Olivia, with Daniel beaming beside them. Talk about excited grandparents; I can't help but grin. Then the aisle clears and my heart stops.

Cole is in his full dress military uniform. He stands strong and tall, hands at his sides. His dark eyes lock with mine, his mouth parts, and his gaze slides down my front stopping at the leg-revealing slit. A devilish grin appears, and my feet move a little faster. Keith pats my hand, giving it a gentle squeeze.

My face hurts from smiling when we finally reach the altar. Keith shakes Cole's hand, giving a little bow to me. I grab his hand and step up on my tiptoes to give him a peck on the cheek. "Thank you," I whisper, and he blinks a few times before he turns and takes his seat.

Cole holds my hand and latches his eyes onto mine. I barely hear the minister speak; I'm so fascinated with this amazing man. He turns my life right side up, and everything makes sense when he's near. He's my life, and now it's going to be official.

Cole flinches, pulling me out of my thoughts. He gives a guilty grin, forcing the minister to repeat his commands. *I can only imagine what he was thinking.* Oh, right, the vows. *Focus, Savannah.*

Cole lets out a puff of air, outing the fact that he's had a brandy. I wonder if he's nervous too. I hear his words.

"I had this recurring dream, where I meet the love of my life, and we spend eternity together. Every day together we would fall deeper and deeper in love. Problem is, as many times as I've dreamed of her, she never had a face." He pauses to collect himself. "Until one night, when I opened a file and found her. I worked like hell to get you, and I'll work like *hell* to keep you. I love you and I always will, Savannah."

Jake hands me a tissue, and I dry my cheeks. I shake my head and try to sort my thoughts. Then I find my voice.

"I always wanted to be Cinderella." I smile shyly. "I wanted to blend in with the colors around me, not be noticed. I certainly never thought I needed a prince. I lost control of my life, I lost hope. Then one day a prince came and took me to his castle. I fell passionately in love. Not only did I *become* Cinderella, but my prince saved me not once, but three times." I step closer and let my lips graze over his smooth jawbone. "I love you, Cole Logan, with all my heart…Fall, Cole, because I *promise* I'll be there to catch you." He reaches out and pulls my head to him, smashing his lips to mine. Everyone breaks into laughter and cheers as he holds me tightly. He reaches deep down in my soul, and any damage left in my heart is finally mended.

***

"Mrs. Logan." Cole's extends a hand and leads me out onto the dance floor, spinning me once and waiting for the music to start. He asked to pick the song for our slow dance. So I'm very eager to hear the song he's chosen. He tugs me closer when the first note is played. My eyes shoot up to his when I hear it. Ed Sheeran's *Thinking Out Loud.* It's perfect. We start moving, and everyone blurs, and I almost forget we are not alone. He looks down and mouths a line from the chorus. I laugh thinking how unique our tale is. *Maybe I should write my story.* He slows the pace toward the end. His hold relaxes, and his chin rests on my head. Figures become bigger and smaller around us. No one matters but us right now.

"I hate your dress," he whispers as I feel him smile into my hair.

"No, you don't."

His laughs, dipping me backward. "Yeah, I don't. You're stunning, Mrs. Logan."

"Mrs. Logan," I repeat. "I like the sound of that."

His eyes light up, remembering the first time I said that.

Jake has me laughing as he dances around me to *Stolen Dance* by Milky Chance. Mark scoops me into his arms and twirls me around in circles. I laugh at his playful face.

"Where's Melanie?" I shout over the music. He sighs and flinches.

"She has decided to head to Chicago for school." Oh no. "So, we broke it off."

"I'm sorry."

He shrugs. "She's a great person, but we got to the 'question part' of our relationship. Where do I live, why do I leave for days on end …you know the drill." His eyes soften and show me his true emotion. "You and Cole are very lucky. Sometimes I think the only way I'll find love is if I change my profession." He smirks a little, pulling his mask back down. "And we all know that won't happen." He clears his throat. "Anyway, it's for the best. I've had someone return to my life that I'm not ready for yet. So until that gets cleared up, I need to stay focused."

"Anything bad?" He nods but doesn't go further, so I leave it be. I think for a moment; I want to choose my words carefully. "This may not count for much, but I know you'll find someone. Maybe not in this town, but she's out there waiting for you to find her."

He leans down and kisses me on the cheek, but before he pulls back his gaze flicks over my shoulder. "Well, that's interesting." He turns me around, and my mouth drops open.

I gasp. "Who is that with Keith?"

"I'm not sure, but I would like to know if she has a sister," Mark mutters, fixing his jacket. I roll my eyes at him, then do a quick scan to find Cole.

My heart nearly bursts when I find him dancing

with Olivia off to the side. She looks so tiny in his huge arms. He's singing her the words to *Love* by Matt White. Her little fingers are over his mouth, and he kisses each one, beaming down at her with so much love. His face lifts, almost as though he can feel me watching. He grins and mouths, "Hi, baby." I wave at them and put a hand on my chest, feeling incredibly complete.

I point over my shoulder to Keith. Cole shakes his head, just as surprised as I am.

"He's free. Keith has secrets. I've seen one once before." Mark shifts to move in front of me, before I can ask what he meant. "Quick, if he's going to spill to anyone, it's you." He pushes me in Keith's direction. I laugh, wondering why Mark cares so much.

"Hey." I tap Keith on the shoulder, and he turns and gives me a look. "Can I have a dance?"

"Mmm hmm," he murmurs quietly. I know he's on to me. Keith's hold is very tense. I can't tell if he's uncomfortable, or if he just doesn't like to dance. "Spit it out, Savi."

I fight my grin, but I really am bad at hiding my emotions. "Who's the pretty woman?"

He drops his eyes to mine. "A date."

"A date?"

"Yes."

"I didn't know you were dating anyone."

"You never asked."

"Okay." I nod, thinking that's fair. I haven't, but Keith isn't someone you talk to about feelings. "What's her name?"

"Annie."

"How did you meet?"

He sighs a little. "She runs the bakery on Mulberry Lane."

I think for a moment. "Is it serious?"

He actually smiles. "No, Savannah, we're just having fun."

"Fun?" I sound like I disapprove, when really I simply find myself feeling protective. I don't want anyone to hurt Keith.

"Yes." He nods and takes a step backward, pulling me along with him. "She's just a friend."

"Okay."

His eyebrow raises as he peers down at me. "Okay?"

"Yes. As long as she's good to you, then I'm happy for you."

"Thanks." He laughs, but I can see that comment hit him deep. He knows I love him.

Daniel interrupts, asking to cut in.

After an hour of dancing, I take a break. The moon is bright, illuminating the thin fabric of the canopy draped above us. Twinkle lights sparkle from the trees, and the lanterns from Cole's proposal hang throughout the forest. The stars are out in the cloudless sky, scattered around the mountains. I step off the wooden dance floor Daniel made, removing my shoes and walking to the edge of the lawn. The grass is cool, and I shiver slightly. They have a spectacular view of the valley. Dipping my head back, I stare up and try to feel her. I recall all the things I love about her…her smile, the sound of her laugh, the way she loved to sing. "I'm happy," I whisper, "really, *really* happy, Mom." I take a deep breath and gather myself. Taking one last view, I turn on my heel to find him watching me a few feet away. His jaw flexes with a twitch of his lips.

"Come home with me?"

The house is surprisingly quiet. Cole takes my hand and leads me downstairs.

"Where are we going?"

He takes our joined hands and gives my diamond wedding band a kiss. "I want to give you my gift." He walks to the last room on the left. I've been in these offices before. He turns to look at me. "This is your room. No one will bother you. It's so you'll never forget." He opens the door and steps out of the way. I grab the doorframe to stabilize myself as I take in the room. "I picked the colors, but June did the rest. If you don't—"

"No," I huff, feeling my voice run off. "It's perfect." I cup my mouth as I step forward. The red soundproof room is huge, with a wall full of books, a seating area filled with gold pillows, and a fireplace. Gracing the center is a beautiful black grand piano.

He pushes off the wall and strolls up to me with a swagger. "I told you I'd give you the world if you came back to me." I want to ask what he means by that, but his hand reaches around my neck while the other slides down my leg, stopping at the garter. "What do we have here?" He drops to his knees to get a better look. He begins to slide his finger under it, but I move his hand to the side.

"Ah, ah, baby, with your teeth."

His eyes turn dark as night. "God, I love you."

My name is Savannah Miller,
and this is my happily ever after.

The End

Acknowledgments

A huge thank you to Corporal George Myatte and Officer Darcy Wood.

About the Author

J. L. Drake was born and raised in Nova Scotia, Canada, later moving to Southern California where she now lives with her husband and two children.

When she is not writing she loves to spend time with her family, travelling or just enjoying a night at home. One thing you might notice in her books is her love of the four seasons. Growing up on the east coast of Canada, the change in the seasons is in her blood and is often mentioned in her writing.

An avid reader of James Patterson, J.L. Drake has often found herself inspired by his many stories of mystery and intrigue. She hopes you will enjoy her books as much as she has enjoyed writing them.

Novels by the Author

Broken (Book One, Broken Trilogy)

Shattered (Book Two, Broken Trilogy)

Mended (Book Three, Broken Trilogy)

What Lurks in the Dark (Book One, Darkness Series)

Bunker 219 (Unleash the Undead, Anthology)

All In (Second Chances Anthology)

Website:
http://www.authorjldrake.com/

Facebook:
https://www.facebook.com/JLDrakeauthor

Twitter:
https://twitter.com/jodildrake_j

Goodreads
http://www.goodreads.com/author/show/8300313.J_L_Drake

Instagram:
@j.l.drake

Pinterest:
JLDrakeAuthor

TSU:
@JLDrake

CPSIA information can be obtained at www.ICGtesting.com
Printed in the USA
LVOW11s2123170815

450538LV00004B/180/P